TALES OF A FOURTH GRADE NOTHING

'Fudge, do you know where Dribble is?' I asked calmly.

Fudge kept smiling.

'Did you take him? Did you, Fudge?' I asked not so calmly.

Fudge giggled and covered his mouth with his hands.

I yelled. 'Where is he? What did you do with my turtle?'

No answer from Fudge. I tried to speak softly. 'Now tell me where Dribble is. I won't be mad if you tell me. Come on, Fudge . . . please.'

Fudge looked up at me. 'In tummy,' he said.

'What do you mean, in tummy?' I asked, narrowing my eyes.

'This one,' Fudge said, rubbing his stomach. 'Dribble in this tummy! Right here!'

I decided to go along with his game. 'Okay. How did he get in there, Fudge?' I asked.

Fudge stood up. He jumped up and down and sang out, 'I ATE HIM . . . ATE HIM . . . ATE HIM!'

Everybody thinks Peter's little brother, Fudge is so cute but as far as Peter's concerned, two-and-a-half year old Farley Drexel Hatcher is a toddling, squawking *flower-eating* NIGHTMARE! Life is sometimes difficult for Peter but at least he's got his tiny green turtle Dribble, to treasure – that is, he has, so long as he can keep his pet and Fudge the monster brother apart!

Other books by Judy Blume include

Otherwise Known as Sheila the Great
Superfudge
Fudge-a-mania

Judy Blume

Growing up in New Jersey, USA, **Judy Blume** used to make up stories while bouncing a ball against the side of her house. It wasn't until she was twenty-seven that she started to write them down. She is now the award-winning author of over twenty books, her work has been translated into fourteen languages, and Judy Blume is a famous name to young readers on both sides of the Atlantic.

When asked to describe how she came to be a writer she says, 'Writing about young people wasn't a conscious decision. It was what I knew best. I wanted to write books about real life, real families, and real feelings.'

When she started writing she was the mother of two small children, and the character of Fudge in *Tales of a Fourth Grade Nothing* is in fact based on her son, Larry, when he was three. Larry has since grown up to be a film maker and recently he directed the film of his mother's book, *Otherwise Known as Sheila the Great*. Judy's daughter Randy is a commercial airline pilot.

Judy Blume lives in New York City with her husband, George Cooper. When she's not working on another book, she enjoys needlepoint and baseball.

TALES OF A FOURTH GRADE NOTHING

– *Judy Blume* –

RANDOM HOUSE
MODERN CLASSICS

A Random House Modern Classic

Published by Random House Children's Books
20 Vauxhall Bridge Road, London SW1V 2SA

A division of Random House UK Ltd
London Melbourne Sydney Auckland
Johannesburg and agencies throughout the world

Copyright © Judy Blume 1972

1 3 5 7 9 10 8 6 4 2

First published by
E P Dutton Publishing Company Inc,
New York 1972
First published in Great Britain by
The Bodley Head Children's Books 1979

This edition 1995

Set in Sabon by SX Composing Ltd, Rayleigh, Essex
Printed and bound in Great Britain by Mackays of
Chatham PLC, Chatham, Kent

RANDOM HOUSE UK Limited Reg. No. 954009

ISBN 0 09 950401 4

*For Larry,
who is a combination of Peter and Fudge,
and for Willie Mae,
who told me about Dribble*

Contents

Contents

– 1 –
The Big Winner

I won Dribble at Jimmy Fargo's birthday party. All the other guys got to take home goldfish in little plastic bags. I won him because I guessed there were three hundred and forty-eight jelly beans in Mrs. Fargo's jar. Really, there were four hundred and twenty-three, she told us later. Still, my guess was closest. 'Peter Warren Hatcher is the big winner!' Mrs. Fargo announced.

At first I felt bad that I didn't get a goldfish too. Then Jimmy handed me a glass bowl. Inside there was some water and three rocks. A tiny green turtle was sleeping on the biggest rock. All the other guys looked at their goldfish. I knew what they were thinking. They wished they could have tiny green turtles too.

I named my turtle Dribble while I was walking home from Jimmy's party. I live at 25 West 68th Street. It's an old apartment building. But it's got one of the best elevators in New York City. There are mirrors all around. You can see yourself from every angle. There's a soft, cushioned bench to sit on if you're too tired to stand. The elevator operator's name is Henry Bevelheimer. He lets us call him Henry because Bevelheimer's very hard to say.

Our apartment's on the twelfth floor. But I don't have to tell Henry. He already knows. He knows everybody in the building. He's that smart! He even knows I'm nine and in fourth grade.

I showed him Dribble right away. 'I won him at a birthday party,' I said.

Henry smiled. 'Your mother's going to be surprised.'

Henry was right. My mother was really surprised. Her mouth opened when I said, 'Just look at what I won at Jimmy Fargo's birthday party.' I held up my tiny green turtle. 'I've already named him . . . Dribble! Isn't that a great name for a turtle?'

My mother made a face. 'I don't like the way he smells,' she said.

'What do you mean?' I asked. I put my nose right down close to him. I didn't smell anything but turtle. *So Dribble smells like turtle,* I thought. *Well, he's supposed to. That's what he is!*

'And I'm not going to take care of him either,' my mother added.

'Of course you're not,' I told her. 'He's my turtle. And I'm the one who's going to take care of him.'

'You're going to change his water and clean out his bowl and feed him and all of that?' she asked.

'Yes,' I said. 'And even more. I'm going to see to it that he's happy!'

This time my mother made a funny noise. Like a groan.

I went into my bedroom. I put Dribble on top of my dresser. I tried to pet him and tell him he would be happy living with me. But it isn't easy to pet a turtle. They aren't soft and furry and they don't lick you or anything. Still, I had my very own pet at last.

Later, when I sat down at the dinner table, my mother said, 'I smell turtle. Peter, go and *scrub* your hands!'

*

Some people might think that my mother is my biggest problem. She doesn't like turtles and she's always telling me to scrub my hands. That doesn't mean just run them under the water. *Scrub* means I'm supposed to use soap and rub my hands together. Then I've got to rinse and dry them. I ought to know by now. I've heard it enough!

But my mother isn't my biggest problem. Neither is my father. He spends a lot of time watching commercials on TV. That's because he's in the advertising business. These days his favourite commercial is the one about Juicy-O. He wrote it himself. And the president of the Juicy-O company liked it so much he sent my father a whole crate of Juicy-O for our family to drink. It tastes like a combination of oranges, pineapples, grapefruits, pears, and bananas. (And if you want to know the truth, I'm getting pretty sick of drinking it.) But Juicy-O isn't my biggest problem either.

My biggest problem is my brother, Farley Drexel Hatcher. He's two-and-a-half years old. Everybody calls him Fudge. I feel sorry for him if he's going to grow up with a name like Fudge, but I don't say a word. It's none of my business.

Fudge is always in my way. He messes up everything he sees. And when he gets mad he throws himself flat on the floor and he screams. *And* he kicks. *And* he bangs his fists. The only time I really like him is when he's sleeping. He sucks four fingers on his left hand and makes a slurping noise.

When Fudge saw Dribble he said, 'Ohhhhh . . . see!'

And I said, 'That's *my* turtle, get it? *Mine!* You don't

touch him.'

Fudge said, 'No touch.' Then he laughed like crazy.

– 2 –
Mr. and Mrs. Juicy-O

One night my father came home from the office all excited. He told us Mr. and Mrs. Yarby were coming to New York. He's the president of the Juicy-O company. He lives in Chicago. I wondered if he'd bring my father another crate of Juicy-O. If he did I'd probably be drinking it for the rest of my life. Just thinking about it was enough to make my stomach hurt.

My father said he invited Mr. and Mrs. Yarby to stay with us. My mother wanted to know why they couldn't stay at a hotel like most people who come to New York. My father said they could. But he didn't want them to. He thought they'd be more comfortable staying with us. My mother said that was about the silliest thing she'd ever heard.

' But she fixed up Fudge's bedroom for our guests. She put fancy sheets and a brand-new blanket on the hide-a-bed. That's a sofa that opens up into a bed at night. It's in Fudge's room because that used to be our den. Before he was born we watched TV in there. And lots of times Grandma slept over on the hide-a-bed. Now we watch TV right in the living room. And Grandma doesn't sleep over very often.

My mother moved Fudge's crib into my room. He's going to get a regular bed when he's three, my mother says. There are a lot of reasons I don't like to sleep in the same room as Fudge. I found that out two months ago when my bedroom was being painted. I had to sleep in Fudge's room for three nights because the paint smell made me cough. For one thing, he talks in his sleep. And if a person didn't know better, a person could get scared. Another thing is that slurping noise he makes. It's true that I like to hear it when I'm awake, but when I'm trying to fall asleep I like things very quiet.

When I complained about having to sleep with Fudge my mother said, 'It's just for two nights, Peter.'

'I'll sleep in the living room,' I suggested. 'On the sofa . . . or even a chair.'

'No,' my mother said. 'You will sleep in your bedroom. In your own bed!'

There was no point in arguing. Mom wasn't going to change her mind.

She spent the day in the kitchen. She really cooked up a storm. She used so many pots and pans Fudge didn't have any left to bang together. And that's one of his favourite pastimes – banging pots and pans together. A person can get an awful headache listening to that racket.

Right after lunch my mother opened up the dinner table. We don't have a separate dining room. When we have company for dinner we eat in one end of the living room. When Mom finished setting the table she put a silver bowl filled with flowers right in the middle. I said, 'Hey, Mom . . . it looks like you're expecting the President or something.'

'Very funny, Peter!' my mother answered.

Sometimes my mother laughs like crazy at my jokes. Other times she pretends not to get them. And then, there are times when I know she gets them but she doesn't seem to like them. This was one of those times. So I decided no more jokes until after dinner.

I went to Jimmy Fargo's for the afternoon. I came home at four o'clock. I found my mother standing over the dinner table mumbling. Fudge was on the floor playing with my father's socks. I'm not sure why he likes socks so much, but if you give him a few pairs he'll play quietly for an hour.

I said, 'Hi, Mom. I'm home.'

'I'm missing two flowers,' my mother said.

I don't know how she noticed that two flowers were missing from her silver bowl. Because there were at least a dozen of them left. But sure enough, when I checked, I saw two stems with nothing on them.

'Don't look at me, Mom,' I said. 'What would I do with two measly flowers?'

So we both looked at Fudge. 'Did you take Mommy's pretty flowers?' my mother asked him.

'No take,' Fudge said. He was chewing on something.

'What's in your mouth?' my mother asked.

Fudge didn't answer.

'Show Mommy!'

'No show,' Fudge said.

'Oh yes!' My mother picked him up and forced his mouth open. She fished out a rose petal.

'What did you do with Mommy's flowers?' She raised her voice. She was really getting upset.

Fudge laughed.

'Tell Mommy!'

'Yum!' Fudge said. 'Yummy yummy yummy!'

'Oh no!' my mother cried, rushing to the telephone. She called Dr. Cone. She told him that Fudge ate two flowers. Dr Cone must have asked what kind, because my mother said, 'Roses, I think. But I can't be sure. One might have been a daisy.'

There was a long pause while my mother listened to whatever Dr. Cone had to say. Then Mom said, 'Thank you, Dr. Cone.' She hung up.

'No more flowers!' she told Fudge. 'You understand?'

'No more,' Fudge repeated. 'No more . . . no more . . . no more.'

My mother gave him a spoonful of peppermint-flavoured medicine. The kind I take when I have stomach pains. Then she carried Fudge off to have his bath.

Leave it to my brother to eat flowers! I wondered how they tasted. *Maybe they're delicious and I don't know it because I've never tasted one,* I thought. I decided to find out. I picked off one petal from a pink rose. I put it in my mouth and tried to chew it up. But I couldn't do it. It tasted awful. I spit it out in the garbage. Well, at least now I knew I wasn't missing anything great!

Fudge ate his supper in the kitchen before our company arrived. While he was eating I heard my mother remind him, 'Fudgie's going to be a good boy tonight. Very good for Daddy's friends.'

'Good,' Fudge said. 'Good boy.'

'That's right!' my mother told him.

I changed and scrubbed up while Fudge finished his supper. I was going to eat with the company. Being nine has its advantages!

My mother was all dressed up by the time my father got home with the Yarbys. You'd never have guessed that

Mom spent most of the day in the kitchen. You'd also never have guessed that Fudge ate two flowers. He was feeling fine. He even smelled nice – like baby powder.

Mrs. Yarby picked him up right away. I knew she would. She looked like a grandmother. That type always makes a big deal out of Fudge. She walked into the living room cuddling him. Then she sat down on the sofa and bounced Fudge around on her lap.

'Isn't he the cutest little boy!' Mrs. Yarby said. 'I just love babies.' She gave him a big kiss on the top of his head. I kept waiting for somebody to tell her Fudge was no baby. But no one did.

My father carried the Yarbys' suitcase into Fudge's room. When he came back he introduced me to our company.

'This is our older son, Peter,' he said to the Yarbys.

'I'm nine and in fourth grade,' I told him.

'How do, Peter,' Mr. Yarby said.

Mrs. Yarby just gave me a nod. She was still busy with Fudge. 'I have a surprise for this dear little boy!' she said. 'It's in my suitcase. Should I go get it?'

'Yes,' Fudge shouted. 'Go get . . . go get!'

Mrs. Yarby laughed, as if that was the best joke she ever heard. 'I'll be right back,' she told Fudge. She put him down and ran off to find her suitcase.

She came back carrying a present tied up with a red ribbon.

'Ohhhh!' Fudge cried, opening his eyes wide. 'Goody!' He clapped his hands.

Mrs. Yarby helped him unwrap his surprise. It was a windup train that made a lot of noise. Every time it bumped into something it turned around and went the other way. Fudge liked it a lot. He likes anything that's noisy.

I said, 'That's a nice train.'

Mrs. Yarby turned to me. 'Oh, I have something for you too uh . . . uh . . .'

'Peter,' I reminded her. 'My name is Peter.'

'Yes. Well, I'll go get it.'

Mrs. Yarby left the room again. This time she came back with a flat package. It was wrapped up too – red ribbon and all. She handed it to me. Fudge stopped playing with his train long enough to come over and see what I got. I took off the paper very carefully in case my mother wanted to save it. And also to show Mrs. Yarby that I'm a lot more careful about things than my brother. I'm not sure she noticed. My present turned out to be a big picture dictionary. The kind I liked when I was about four years old. My old one is in Fudge's bookcase now.

'I don't know much about big boys,' Mrs. Yarby said. 'So the lady in the store said a nice book would be a good idea.'

A nice book would have been a good idea, I thought. *But a picture dictionary! That's for babies!* I've had my own regular dictionary since I was eight. But I knew I had to be polite so I said, 'Thank you very much. It's just what I've always wanted.'

'I'm so glad!' Mrs. Yarby said. She let out a long sigh and sat back on the sofa.

My father offered the Yarbys a drink.

'Good idea . . . good idea,' Mr. Yarby said.

'What'll it be?' my father asked.

'What'll it be?' Mr. Yarby repeated, laughing. 'What do you think, Hatcher? It'll be Juicy-O! That's all we ever drink. Good for your health!' Mr. Yarby pounded his chest.

'Of course!' my father said, like he knew it all along. 'Juicy-O for everyone!' my father told my mother. She went into the kitchen to get it.

While my father and Mr. Yarby were discussing Juicy-O, Fudge disappeared. Just as my mother served everyone a glass of Mr. Yarby's favourite drink he came back. He was carrying a book – my old, worn-out picture dictionary. The same as the one the Yarbys just gave me.

'See,' Fudge said, climbing up on Mrs. Yarby's lap. 'See book.'

I wanted to vanish, I think my mother and father did too.

'See book!' Now Fudge held it up over his head.

'I can use another one,' I explained. 'I really can. That old one is falling apart.' I tried to laugh.

'It's returnable,' Mrs. Yarby said. 'It's silly to keep it if you already have one.' She sounded insulted. Like it was my fault she brought me something I already had.

'MINE!' Fudge said. He closed the book and held it tight against his chest. 'MINE . . . MINE . . . MINE . . .'

'It's the thought that counts,' my mother said. 'It was so nice of you to think of our boys.' Then she turned to Fudge. 'Put the book away now, Fudgie.'

'Isn't it Fudgie's bedtime?' my father hinted.

'Oh yes, I think it is,' my mother said, scooping him up. 'Say goodnight, Fudgie.'

'Goodnight Fudgie!' my brother said, waving at us.

Fudge was supposed to fall asleep before we sat down to dinner. But just in case, my mother put a million little toys in his crib to keep him busy. I don't know who my mother thought she was fooling. Because we all knew that Fudge can climb out of his crib any old time he wants to.

He stayed away until we were in the middle of our roast beef. Then he came in carrying Dribble's bowl. He walked right up to Mrs. Yarby. He thought she was his new friend. 'See,' he said, holding Dribble under her nose. 'See Dribble.'

Mrs. Yarby shrieked. 'Ohhhh! I can't stand reptiles. Get that thing away from me!'

Fudge looked disappointed. So he showed Dribble to Mr. Yarby. 'See,' he said.

'HATCHER!' Mr. Yarby boomed. 'Make him get that thing out of here!'

I wondered why Mr. Yarby called my father 'Hatcher'. Didn't he know his first name was Warren? And I didn't like the way Mr. and Mrs. Yarby both called Dribble a 'thing'.

I jumped up. 'Give him to me!' I told Fudge. I took Dribble and his bowl and marched into my room. I inspected my turtle all over. He seemed all right. I didn't want to make a big scene in front of our company but I was mad! I mean *really* mad! That kid knows he's not allowed to touch my turtle!

'Peter,' my father called, 'come and finish your dinner.'

When I got back to the table I heard Mrs. Yarby say, 'It must be interesting to have children. We never had any ourselves.'

'But if we did,' Mr. Yarby told my father, 'we'd teach them some manners. I'm a firm believer in old-fashioned good manners!'

'So are we, Howard,' my father said in a weak voice.

I thought Mr. Yarby had a lot of nerve to hint that we had no manners. Didn't I pretend to like their dumb old picture dictionary? If that isn't good manners, then I don't know what is!

My mother excused herself and carried Fudge back to my room. I guess she put him into his crib again. I hoped she told him to keep his hands off my things.

We didn't hear from him again until dessert. Just as my mother was pouring the coffee he ran in wearing my rubber gorilla mask from last Hallowe'en. It's a very real-looking mask. I guess that's why Mrs. Yarby screamed so loud. If she hadn't made so much noise my mother probably wouldn't have spilled the coffee all over the floor.

My father grabbed Fudge and pulled the gorilla mask off him. 'That's not funny, Fudge!' he said.

'Funny,' Fudge laughed. 'Funny, funny, funny Fudgie!'

'Yes sir, Hatcher!' Mr. Yarby said. 'Old-fashioned manners!'

By that time I'm sure my father was sorry the Yarbys weren't staying at a hotel.

I finally got to bed at ten. Fudge was in his crib slurping away. I thought I'd never fall asleep! But I guess I did. I woke up once, when Fudge started babbling. He said, 'Boo-ba-mum-mum-ha-ba-shi.' Whatever that means. I didn't even get scared. I whispered, 'Shut up!' And he did.

Early the next morning I felt something funny on my arm. At first I didn't wake up. I just felt this little tickle.

I thought it was part of my dream. But then I had the feeling somebody was staring at me. So I opened my eyes.

Fudge was standing over me and Dribble was crawling around on my arm. I guess Fudge could tell I was about ready to kill him because he bent down and kissed me. That's what he does when my mother's angry at him. He thinks nobody can resist him when he makes himself so lovable. And a lot of times it works with my mother. But not with me! I jumped up, put Dribble back into his bowl, and smacked Fudge on his backside. *Hard*. He hollered.

My father came running into my room. He was still in his pyjamas.

He whispered, 'What's going on in here?'

I pointed at Fudge and he pointed at me.

My father picked up my brother and carried him off. 'Go back to sleep, Peter,' he said. 'It's only six o'clock in the morning.'

I fell asleep for another hour, then woke up to an awful noise. It was Fudge playing with his new train. It woke up everyone, including the Yarbys. But this time there was nobody they could blame. They were the ones who gave Fudge the train in the first place.

Breakfast was a very quiet affair. Nobody had much to say. Mr. Yarby drank two glasses of Juicy-O. Then he told my father that he and Mrs. Yarby had their suitcase packed. They were leaving for a hotel as soon as breakfast was over.

My father said he understood. That the apartment was too small for so many people. My mother didn't say anything.

When Mr. Yarby went into Fudge's bedroom to pick up his suitcase his voice boomed. 'HATCHER!'

My father ran toward the bedroom. My mother and Mrs. Yarby followed him. I followed them. When we got there we saw Fudge sitting on the Yarbys' suitcase. He had decorated it with about one hundred green stamps. The kind my mother gets at the supermarket.

'See,' Fudge said. 'See . . . pretty.' He laughed. Nobody else did. Then he licked the last green stamp and stuck it right in the middle of the suitcase. 'All gone!' Fudge sang, holding up his hands.

It took my mother half an hour to peel off her trading stamps and clean up the Yarbys' suitcase.

The next week my father came home from the office and collected all the cans of Juicy-O in our house. He dumped them into the garbage. My mother felt bad that my father had lost such an important account. But my father told her not to worry. Juicy-O wasn't selling very well at the stores. Nobody seemed to like the combination of oranges, grapefruits, pineapples, pears, and bananas.

'You know, Dad,' I said. 'I only drank Juicy-O to be polite. I really hated it!'

'You know something funny, Peter?' my father said. 'I thought it was pretty bad myself!'

– 3 –
The Family Dog

Nobody ever came right out and said that Fudge was the reason my father lost the Juicy-O account. But I thought about it. My father said he was glad to be rid of Mr. Yarby. Now he could spend more time on his other clients – like the Toddle-Bike company. My father is in charge of their new TV commercial.

I though maybe he could use me in it since I know how to stand on my head. But he said he wasn't planning on having any head-standers in the commercial.

I learned to stand on my head in gym class. I'm pretty good at it too. I can stay up for as long as three minutes. I showed my mother, my father, and Fudge how I can do it right in the living room. They were all impressed. Especially Fudge. He wanted to do it too. So I turned him upside down and tried to teach him. But he always tumbled over backwards.

Right after I learned to stand on my head Fudge stopped eating. He did it suddenly. One day he ate fine and the next day nothing. 'No eat!' he told my mother.

She didn't pay too much attention to him until the third day. When he still refused to eat she got upset. 'You've got to eat, Fudgie,' she said. 'You want to grow up to be big and strong, don't you?'

'No grow!' Fudge said.

That night my mother told my father how worried she was about Fudge. So my father did tricks for him while my mother stood over his chair trying to get some food into his mouth. But nothing worked. Not even juggling oranges.

Finally my mother got the brilliant idea of me standing on my head while she fed Fudge. I wasn't very excited about standing on my head in the kitchen. The floor is awfully hard in there. But my mother begged me. She said, 'It's very important for Fudge to eat. Please help us, Peter.'

So I stood on my head. When Fudge saw me upside down he clapped his hands and laughed. When he laughs he opens his mouth. That's when my mother stuffed some baked potato into it.

But the next morning I put my foot down. 'No! I don't want to stand on my head in the kitchen. Or anywhere else!' I added, 'And if I don't hurry I'll be late for school.'

'Don't you care if your brother starves?'

'No!' I told her.

'Peter! What an awful thing to say.'

'Oh . . . he'll eat when he gets hungry. Why don't you just leave him alone!'

That afternoon when I came home from school I found my brother on the kitchen floor playing with boxes of cereals and raisins and dried apricots. My mother was begging him to eat.

'No, no, no!' Fudge shouted. He made a terrible mess, dumping everything on the floor.

'Please stand on your head, Peter,' my mother said. 'It's the only way he'll eat.'

'No!' I told her. 'I'm not going to stand on my head any more.' I went into my room and slammed the door. I played with Dribble until suppertime. Nobody ever worries about me the way they worry about Fudge. If I decided not to eat they'd probably never even notice!

That night during dinner Fudge hid under the kitchen table. He said, 'I'm a doggie. Woof . . . woof . . . woof!'

It was hard to eat with him under the table pulling on my legs. I waited for my father to say something. But he didn't.

Finally my mother jumped up. 'I know,' she said. 'If Fudgie's a doggie he wants to eat on the floor! Right?'

If you ask me Fudge never even thought about that. But he liked the idea a lot. He barked and nodded his head. So my mother fixed his plate and put it under the table. Then she reached down and petted him, like he was a real dog.

My father said, 'Aren't we carrying this a little too far?'

My mother didn't answer.

Fudge ate two bites of his dinner.

My mother was satisfied.

After a week of having him eat under the table I felt like we really did have a family dog. I thought how great it would be if we could trade in Fudge for a nice cocker spaniel. That would solve all my problems. I'd walk him and feed him and play with him. He could even sleep on the edge of my bed at night. But of course that was wishful thinking. My brother is here to stay. And there's nothing much I can do about it.

Grandma came over with a million ideas about getting Fudge to eat. She tricked him by making milk shakes in the blender. When Fudge wasn't looking she threw in an egg. Then she told him if he drank it all up there would be a surprise in the bottom of the glass. The first time he believed her. He finished his milk shake. But all he saw was an empty glass. There wasn't any surprise! Fudge got so mad he threw the glass down. It smashed into little pieces. After that Grandma left.

The next day my mother dragged Fudge to Dr. Cone's office. He told her to leave him alone. That Fudge would eat when he got hungry.

I reminded my mother that I'd told her the same thing – and for free! But I guess my mother didn't believe either one of us because she took Fudge to see three more doctors. None of them could find a thing wrong with my brother. One doctor even suggested that my mother cook Fudge his favourite foods.

So that night my mother broiled lamb chops just for Fudge. The rest of us ate stew. She served him the two little lamb chops on his plate under the table. Just the smell of them was enough to make my stomach growl. I thought it was mean of my mother to make them for Fudge and not for me.

Fudge looked at his lamb chops for a few minutes. Then he pushed his plate away. 'No!' he said. 'No chops!'

'Fudgie . . . you'll starve!' my mother cried. 'You *must* eat!'

'No chops! Corn Flakes,' Fudge said. 'Want Corn Flakes!'

My mother ran to get the cereal for Fudge. 'You can eat the chops if you want them, Peter,' she told me.

I reached down and helped myself to the lamb chops. My mother handed Fudge his bowl of cereal. But he didn't eat it. He sat at my feet and looked up at me. He watched me eat his chops.

'*Eat your cereal!*' my father said.

'NO! NO EAT CEREAL!' Fudge yelled.

My father was really mad. His face turned bright red. He said, 'Fudge, you will eat that cereal or you will wear it!'

This was turning out to be fun after all, I thought. And the lamb chops were really tasty. I dipped the bone in some Ketchup and chewed away.

Fudge messed around with his cereal for a minute. Then he looked at my father and said, 'NO EAT . . . NO EAT . . . NO EAT!'

My father wiped his mouth with his napkin, pushed back his chair, and got up from the table. He picked up the bowl of cereal in one hand, and Fudge in the other. He carried them both into the bathroom. I went along, nibbling on a bone, to see what was going to happen.

My father stood Fudge in the bath and dumped the whole bowl of cereal right over his head. Fudge screamed. He sure can scream loud.

My father motioned for me to go back to the kitchen. He joined us in a minute. We sat down and finished our dinner. Fudge kept on screaming. My mother wanted to go to him but my father told her to stay where she was. He'd had enough of Fudge's monkey business at meal times.

I think my mother really was relieved that my father had taken over. For once my brother got what he deserved. And I was glad!

The next day Fudge sat at the table again. In his little red booster chair, where he belongs. He ate everything my mother put in front of him. 'No more doggie,' he told us.

And for a long time after that his favourite expression
was 'eat it or wear it!'

– 4 –
My Brother the Bird

We live near Central Park. On nice days I like to play there after school. I'm allowed to walk over by myself as long as I'm going to be with friends. My mother doesn't want me hanging around the park alone.

For one thing, Jimmy Fargo has been mugged three times – twice for his bicycle and once for his money. Only he didn't have any to give the muggers.

I've never been mugged. But sooner or later I probably will be. My father's told me what to do. Give the muggers whatever they want and try not to get hit on the head.

Sometimes, after you're mugged, you get to go to police headquarters. You look at a bunch of pictures of crooks to see if you can recognize the guys that mugged you.

I think it would be neat to look at all those pictures. It's not that I want to get mugged, because that could be really scary. It's just that Jimmy Fargo's always talking about his visit to police headquarters.

My father got mugged once in a subway by two girls and a guy. They took his wallet and his briefcase. He still travels around by subways but my mother doesn't. She sticks to buses and taxis.

Both my mother and my father are always warning me never to talk to strangers in the park. Because a lot of dope-pushers hang around there. But taking dope is even dumber than smoking, so nobody's going to hook me!

We live on the west side of the park. If I want to get to the zoo and the pony carts I have to walk all the way through to the east side. Sometimes my mother walks across the park with Fudge. He likes the animals a lot. Especially the monkeys. He also likes the helium-filled balloons. But as soon as my mother buys him one he lets it go. I think he likes to see it float up in the sky. My mother says that's a waste of money and she's not going to buy him any more balloons until he promises not to let go.

On Sundays the park is closed to traffic and you can ride your bicycle all over without worrying about being run down by some crazy driver. Even Fudge can ride. He has a little blue Toddle-Bike, a present from my father's client. And when he's riding he makes motorcycle noises. 'Vroom-vroom-vroom!' he yells.

In the fall the leaves turn darker and drop off the trees. Sometimes there are big leaf piles on the ground. It's fun to jump around in them. I never saw bright red, yellow, and orange leaves until the day my father took us for a drive in the country. The reason the leaves don't turn bright colours in New York is the air pollution. And that's too bad. Because yellow and orange and red leaves really look neat!

One nice sunny afternoon I called for Jimmy Fargo and we went to the park. Jimmy is the only kid on my block who's in my class at school. Unless you count Sheila. And I don't! She lives in my building, on the tenth floor. Henry, the elevator operator, is always making jokes about me and Sheila. He thinks we like each other.

The truth is, I can't stand her. She's a real know-it-all. But I've discovered that most girls are!

The worst thing about Sheila is the way she's always trying to touch me. And when she does she yells, 'Peter's got the cooties! Peter's got the cooties!' I don't believe in cooties any more. When I was in second grade, I used to examine myself to see if I had them. But I never found any. By fourth grade most kids give up on cooties. But not Sheila. She's still going strong. So I have to keep a safe distance from her.

My mother thinks Sheila is the greatest. 'She's so smart,' my mother says. 'And some day she's going to be a real beauty.' Now that's the funniest! Because Sheila looks a lot like the monkeys that Fudge is so crazy about. So maybe she'll look beautiful to some ape! *But never to me.*

Me and Jimmy have this special group of rocks where we like to play when we're in the park. We play secret agent up there. Jimmy can imitate all kinds of foreign accents. Probably because his father's a part-time actor. When he's not acting he teaches a class at City College.

Today, when we got to our rocks, who should be perched up there but Sheila. She was pretending to read a book. But I think she was just waiting for me and Jimmy. To find out what we'd do when we found her on our own personal rocks.

'Hey, Sheila!' I said. 'Those are our rocks.'

'Says who?' she asked.

'Come on, Sheila,' Jimmy said, climbing up. 'You know me and Peter hang out here.'

'Too bad for you!' Sheila said.

'Oh, Sheila!' I shouted. 'Go and find yourself another rock!'

'I like this one,' she said, as if she owned the park. 'So why don't you two go find another rock?'

Just then who should come tearing down the path but Fudge. My mother was right behind him hollering, 'Fudgie . . . wait for Mommy!'

But when Fudge gets going he doesn't wait for anybody. He was after some pigeons. 'Birdie . . . here birdie,' he called. That brother of mine loves birds. But he can't get it through his head that the birds aren't about to let him catch them.

'Hi, Mom,' I said.

My mother stopped running. 'Peter! Am I glad to see you. I can't keep up with Fudge.'

'Mrs. Hatcher . . . Mrs. Hatcher,' Sheila called, scrambling down from our rock, 'I'll watch Fudge for you. I'll take very good care of him. Can I, Mrs. Hatcher? Oh please!' Sheila jumped up and down and begged some more.

Jimmy gave me an elbow in the ribs. He thought that my mother would let Sheila watch Fudge and then we'd be rid of her. We'd be free to play secret agent. But Jimmy didn't know that my mother would never trust Sheila with her dear little boy.

Fudge, in the meantime, was screaming. 'Come back, birdies . . . come back to Fudge!'

Then my mother did a strange thing. She checked her watch and said, 'You know, I do have to run back to the apartment. I forgot to turn on the oven. Do you really think you could keep an eye on Fudge for just ten minutes?'

'Of course I can, Mrs. Hatcher,' Sheila said. 'I know all about baby-sitting from my sister.'

Sheila's sister Libby is in seventh grade. She's about as beautiful as Sheila. The only difference is, she's bigger.

My mother hesitated. 'I don't know,' she said. 'I've never left Fudge before.' She looked at me. 'Peter . . .'

'What?'

'Will you and Jimmy help Sheila watch Fudge while I run home for a minute?'

'Oh, Mom! Do we have to?'

'Please, Peter. I'll be right back. I'll feel better if all three of you are watching him.'

'What do you say?' I asked Jimmy.

'Sure,' he answered. 'Why not?'

'But I'm in charge of Fudgie, aren't I?' Sheila asked my mother.

'Well, I guess so,' my mother said to Sheila. 'You probably do know more about baby-sitting. Why don't you all take Fudge over to the playground? Then I'll know where to find you.'

'Swell, Mrs. Hatcher!' Sheila said. 'Don't you worry, Fudgie will be just fine.'

My mother turned to Fudge. 'Now you be a good boy for ten minutes. Mommy will be right back. Okay?'

'Good boy!' Fudge said. 'Good . . . good . . . good . . .'

As soon as my mother was gone Fudge took off. 'Can't catch me!' he hollered. 'Can't catch Fudgie!'

'Go get him, Sheila,' I said. 'You're in charge, remember?'

Me and Jimmy horsed around while Sheila ran after Fudge.

When she caught him we decided we'd better go to the

playground like my mother said. It was a lot easier to keep an eye on him in a smaller place. Anyway, Fudge likes to climb on the jungle gym and that way he can't get lost.

As soon as we got to the playground Sheila started chasing me. 'Peter's got the cooties! Peter's got the cooties!' she yelled.

'Cut that out!' I said.

So she chased Jimmy. 'Jimmy's got the cooties! Jimmy's got the cooties!'

Me and Jimmy decided to fight back. So what if she's a girl? She started it! We grabbed her by the arms. She squirmed and tried to get away from us, but we wouldn't let go. We hollered really loud. 'Sheila's got the cooties! Sheila's got the cooties!'

All three of us were so busy fooling around that we didn't notice Fudge up on the jungle gym until he called 'Pee-tah . . . Pee-tah . . .' That's how he says my name.

'What?' I asked.

'See . . . see . . .' Fudge flapped his arms around. 'Fudgie's a birdie! Fudgie's a birdie! Fly, birdie . . . fly . . .'

That crazy kid! I thought, running to the jungle gym with Jimmy and Sheila right behind me.

But it was too late. Fudge already found out he didn't have wings. He fell to the ground. He was screaming and crying and his face was a mess of blood. I couldn't even tell where the blood was coming from at first. Then Jimmy handed me his handkerchief. I don't know how clean it was but it was better than nothing. I mopped some blood off Fudge's face.

Sheila cried, 'It wasn't my fault. Honest, it wasn't.'

'Oh shut up!' I told her.

'He's really a mess,' Jimmy said, inspecting Fudge. 'And his teeth are gone too.'

'What are you talking about?' I asked Jimmy.

'Look in his mouth,' Jimmy said. 'Now, while he's screaming. See . . . he's got a big space where he used to have his front teeth.'

'Oh no!' Sheila screamed. 'He's right! Fudgie's teeth are gone!'

Fudge stopped crying for a minute. 'All gone?' he asked.

'Open your mouth wide,' I said.

He did and I looked in. It was true. His top two front teeth were missing.

'My mother's going to kill you, Sheila!' I said. Was I glad I wasn't left in charge of my brother.

Sheila cried louder. 'But it was an accident. He did it himself . . . himself . . .'

'You better find his teeth,' I said.

'Where should I look?' Sheila asked.

'On the ground, stupid!'

Sheila crawled around looking for Fudge's teeth while I tried to clean him up some more. 'See,' Fudge said, showing me all his wounds. 'Boo-boo here. And here. More boo-boo here.' His knees and elbows were all grazed.

'I'm going to get your mother,' Jimmy hollered, running out of the playground.

'Good idea!' I called.

'I just can't find them,' Sheila said.

'Well, keep looking!' I yelled.

'Honestly, Peter, there aren't any teeth here!'

'All gone?' Fudge asked again.

'Not all,' I told him. 'Just two.'

Fudge started to scream. 'Want my teeth! Want my teeth!'

Jimmy must have met my mother on her way back to the park because it only took about two minutes for her to get there. By that time a whole crowd of kids had gathered around us. Most of them were crawling on the ground like Sheila, looking for Fudge's teeth.

My mother picked up Fudge. 'Oh my baby! My precious! My little love!' She kissed him all over. 'Show Mommy where it hurts.'

Fudge showed her all his boo-boos. Then he said, 'All gone!'

'What's all gone?' my mother asked.

'His top two front teeth,' I said.

'Oh no!' my mother cried. 'Oh, my poor little angel!'

Sheila sniffled and said, 'I just can't find them, Mrs. Hatcher. I've looked everywhere but Fudge's teeth are gone!'

'He must have swallowed them,' my mother said, looking into Fudge's mouth.

'Oh, Mrs. Hatcher! How awful. I'm sorry . . . I'm really very sorry,' Sheila cried. 'What will happen to him?'

'He'll be all right, Sheila,' my mother said. 'I'm sure it was an accident. Nobody's blaming you.'

Sheila started bawling again.

My mother said, 'Let's go home now.'

I thought my mother was being pretty easy on Sheila. After all, *she* was left in charge. When we got home Mom washed Fudge's cuts and scrapes with peroxide.

Then she called Dr. Cone. He told her to take Fudge to our dentist. So my mother called Dr. Brown's office and made an appointment for the next day.

When that was done she gave Fudge some socks to play with. I went into the kitchen to have a glass of juice. My mother followed me. 'Peter Warren Hatcher!' she said. 'I'm sorry that I can't trust you for just ten minutes!'

'Me?' I asked. 'Trust me? What's this got to do with me?'

My mother raised her voice. 'I left your brother with you for ten minutes and just look at what happened. I'm disgusted with you!'

'It was Sheila's fault,' I said. 'You said Sheila was in charge. So how come you're mad at me and not at Sheila?'

'I just am!' my mother shouted.

I ran to my room and slammed the door. I watched Dribble walk around on his favourite rock. 'My mother's the meanest mother in the whole world!' I told my turtle. 'She loves Fudge more than me. She doesn't even *love* me any more. She doesn't even *like* me. Maybe I'm not her real son. Maybe somebody left me in a basket on her doorstep. My real mother's probably a beautiful princess. I'll bet she'd like to have me back. Nobody needs me around here . . . that's for sure!'

I didn't eat much supper that night and I had a lot of trouble falling asleep.

The next morning my mother came into my room and sat down on my bed. I didn't look at her.

'Peter,' she said.

I didn't answer.

'Peter, I said some things yesterday that I didn't really mean.'

I looked at her. 'Honest?' I asked.

'Yes . . . you see . . . I was very upset over Fudge's accident and I had to blame somebody. So I picked on you.'

'Yes,' I said. 'You sure did.'

'It wasn't your fault though. I know that. It was an accident. It could have happened even if I had been in the playground myself.'

'He wanted to fly,' I said. 'He thought he was a bird.'

'I don't think he'll try to fly again,' my mother said.

'Me neither,' I told her.

Then we both laughed and I knew she was my real mother after all.

– 5 –
The Birthday Bash

I got used to the way Fudge looked without his top front teeth. He looked like a very small first grader. Dr. Brown, our dentist, said he'd have to wait until he was six or seven to get his grown-up teeth. I started calling him Fang because when he smiles all you can see are the top two side teeth next to the big space. So it looks like he has fangs.

My mother didn't like that. 'I want you to stop calling him Fang,' she told me.

'What should I call him?' I asked. 'Farley Drexel?'

'Just plain Fudge will be fine,' my mother said.

'What's wrong with Farley Drexel?' I asked. 'How come you named him that if you don't like it?'

'I like it fine,' my mother said. 'But right now we call him Fudge. Not Farley . . . not Drexel . . . and *not* Fang!'

'What's wrong with Fang?' I asked. 'I think it sounds neat.'

'Fang is an insult!'

'Oh . . . come on, Mom! He doesn't even know what a fang is!'

'But *I* know Peter. And *I* don't like it.'

'Okay . . . okay . . .' I promised never to call my brother Fang again.

But secretly, whenever I look at him, I think it. *My brother, Fang Hatcher!* Nobody can stop me from thinking. My mind is my own.

Fudge is going to be three years old. My mother said he should have a birthday party with some of his friends. He plays with three other little kids who live in our building. There's Jennie, Ralph, and Sam. My mother invited them to Fudge's party. Grandma said she'd come over to help. My father couldn't make it. He had a Saturday business appointment. I wanted to go to Jimmy Fargo's but my mother said she needed me to supervise the games. The kids were invited from one until two-thirty.

'That's only an hour and a half,' my mother reminded me. 'That's not so bad, is it Peter?'

'I don't know yet,' I told her. 'Ask me later.'

The kitchen table was set up for the party. The cloth and napkins and paper plates and cups all matched. They had pictures of Superman on them.

Right before party time Grandma tried to change Fudge into his new suit. But he screamed his head off about it. 'No suit! No suit! NO . . . NO . . . NO!'

My mother tried to reason with him. 'It's your birthday, Fudgie. All your friends are coming. You want to look like a big boy, don't you?' While she was talking to him she managed to get him into his shirt and pants. But he wouldn't let her put on his shoes. He kicked and carried on until my mother and grandmother were both black and blue. Finally they decided as long as he was in his suit his feet didn't matter. So he wore his old bedroom slippers.

Ralph arrived first. He's really fat. And he isn't even four years old. He doesn't say much either. He grunts and grabs a lot, though. Usually his mouth is stuffed full of something.

So the first thing Ralph did was wander into the kitchen. He looked around for something to eat. But Grandma was guarding the place. She kept telling him 'No . . . No . . . must wait until the other children come.'

Jennie arrived next. She was wearing little white gloves and party shoes. She even carried a handbag. Besides that she had on dirty jeans and an old sweater. Her mother apologized for her clothes but said she couldn't do anything with Jennie lately – especially since she had taken to biting.

'What does she bite?' I asked, thinking about furniture or toys or stuff like that.

'She bites people,' Jennie's mother said. 'But you don't have to worry about it unless her teeth go through the skin. Otherwise it's perfectly safe.'

I thought, *poor old Fudge! He can't even bite back since he hasn't got any top front teeth*. I looked at Jennie. She seemed so innocent. It was hard to believe she was a vampire.

Sam came last. He carried a big present for Fudge but he was crying. 'It's just a stage he's going through,' his mother explained. 'Everything scares him. Especially birthday parties. But he'll be fine. Won't you, Sam?'

Sam grabbed onto his mother's leg and screamed, 'Take me home! Take me home!' Somehow Sam's mother untangled herself from Sam's grip and left.

So at five after one we were ready to begin. We had an eater, a biter, and a crier. I thought that two-thirty would never come. I also thought my mother was slightly crazy for dreaming up the party in the first place. 'Doesn't Fudge have any normal friends?' I whispered.

'There's nothing wrong with Fudgie's friends!' my

mother whispered back. 'All small children are like that.'

Grandma got them seated around the kitchen table. She put a party hat on each kid's head. Sam screamed, 'Get it off! Get it off!' But the others wore their hats and didn't complain. My mother snapped a picture of them with her new camera.

Then Grandma turned off the lights and my mother lit the candles on Fudge's cake. It had chocolate frosting and big yellow roses. I led the singing of 'Happy Birthday.' My mother carried the cake across the kitchen to the party table and set it down in front of Fudge.

Sam cried, 'Too dark! Too dark!' So Grandma had to turn on the kitchen lights before Fudge blew out his candles. When he had finished blowing he reached out and grabbed a rose off his cake. He shoved it into his mouth.

'Oh Fudge!' my mother said. 'Look what you did.'

But Grandma said, 'It's his birthday. He can do whatever he wants!'

So Fudge reached over and grabbed a second rose.

I guess fat Ralph couldn't stand seeing Fudge eat those yellow roses because he grabbed one, too. By that time the cake looked pretty messy. My mother, finally coming to her senses, took the cake away and sliced it up.

Each kid got a Dixie cup, a small piece of cake, and some milk. But Jennie hollered, 'Where's my rose? Want one too!' Because her slice of birthday cake didn't happen to have one.

My mother explained that the roses were only decorations and there weren't enough to go around. Jennie seemed to accept that. But when Grandma stood over her to help open her Dixie, Jennie bit her on the hand.

'She bit me!' Grandma cried.

'Did it break the skin?' my mother asked.

'No . . . I don't think so,' Grandma said, checking.

'Good. Then it's nothing to worry about,' my mother told her.

Grandma went into the bathroom to put some medicine on it anyway. She wasn't taking any chances.

Ralph was the first one to finish his food. 'More . . . more . . . more!' he sang, holding up his empty plate.

'I don't think you should give him any more,' I whispered to my mother. 'Look how fat he is now!'

'Oh, Peter . . . this is a party. Let him eat whatever he wants.'

'Okay,' I said. 'Why should I care how fat he gets?'

My mother served Ralph a second piece of cake. He threw up right after he finished it.

Me and Grandma took the kids into the living room while my mother cleaned up the mess.

Grandma told Fudge he could open his presents while his friends watched. Jennie brought him a musical jack-in-the-box. When you turn the handle around it plays 'Pop Goes the Weasel.' When you reach the part of the song about Pop, the top opens and a funny clown jumps up. Fudge loved it. He clapped his hands and laughed and laughed. But Sam started to scream, 'No! No more. Take it away!' He hid his face in his hands and wouldn't look up until Grandma promised to put the jack-in-the-box in another room.

Fudge opened Ralph's present next. It was a little windup car that ran all over the floor. I kind of liked it myself. So did Ralph. Because he grabbed it away from Fudge and said, 'MINE.'

'No!' Fudge shouted. 'MINE.'

When my mother heard the racket she ran in from the kitchen. She explained to Ralph that he had brought the car to Fudge because it was *his* birthday. But Ralph wouldn't listen. I guess my mother was afraid he might throw up again, and this time on the living room rug. So she begged Fudge to let Ralph play with the car for a few minutes. But Ralph kept screaming it was *his* car. So Fudge started to cry. Finally, my mother took the car away and said, 'Let's see what Sam brought you.'

Fudge liked that idea. He forgot about the little car as he ripped the paper and ribbon off Sam's package. It turned out to be a big picture dictionary. The same kind the Yarbys brought me a couple of months ago. Fudge got mad when he saw it.

'No!' he yelled. 'NO MORE BOOK!' He threw it across the room.

'Fudge! That's terrible,' my mother said. 'You mustn't do that to the nice book.'

'No book!' Fudge said.

Sam cried, 'He doesn't like it. He doesn't like my present. I want to go home . . . I want to go home!'

Grandma tried to comfort Sam while my mother picked up the book. She gathered the wrapping paper and ribbons and cards together. Fudge didn't even look at any of the birthday cards. Oh well, he can't read, so I guess it doesn't make any difference.

'Peter,' my mother said, 'let's start the games . . . now . . . quick!'

I checked the time. I hoped the party was almost over. But no, it was only one-thirty. Still an hour to go. I went into my room where I had blown up a lot of balloons.

My mother has this party book and it says three-year-olds like to dance around with balloons. When I got back to the living room Mom started the record player and I handed each kid a balloon.

But they just stood there looking at me. I thought, *either the guy who wrote that party book is crazy or I am!*

'Show them how, Peter,' my mother said. 'Take a balloon and demonstrate.'

I felt like one of the world's great living fools dancing around with a balloon, but it worked. As soon as the kids saw me doing it, they started dancing too. And the more they danced the more they liked it. Until Jennie's balloon popped. That nearly scared Sam right out of his mind. He started yelling and crying. Fortunately I had blown up two dozen balloons. I was hoping they'd dance around the rest of the afternoon.

Fudge got the idea of jumping up and down on the furniture. The others liked that too. So instead of dancing with their balloons, that's what they did. And soon they were running from room to room, yelling and laughing and having a great time.

Then the doorbell rang. It was Mrs. Rudder. She lives in the apartment right under us. She wanted to know what was going on. She said it sounded like her ceiling was about to crash in on her any second.

My mother explained that Fudge was having a little birthday party and wouldn't she like to stay for a piece of cake? Sometimes my mother is really clever! So Grandma entertained Mrs. Rudder in the kitchen while Fudge and his buddies jumped up and down on his new bed.

It was delivered this morning. Fudge hasn't even slept in it yet. So naturally when my mother found out what they were up to, she was mad. 'Stop it right now!' she said.

'New bed . . . big boy!' Fudge told her. Was he proud!

'You won't have a new-big-boy-bed for long if you don't stop jumping on it,' my mother told him. 'I know . . . let's all sit down on the floor and hear a nice story.' My mother selected a picture book from Fudge's bookshelf.

'I heard that one!' Jennie said when she saw the cover.

'All right,' my mother told her. 'Let's hear this one.' She held up another book.

'I heard that one too,' Jennie said.

I think my mother was starting to lose her patience. But she chose a third book and said, 'We'll all enjoy this one even if we know it by heart. And if we *do* know it by heart . . . well, we can say it together.'

That's just what Jennie did. And when my mother skipped a page by mistake Jennie was right there to remind her. If you ask me, my mother felt like biting Jennie by that time!

When the story was over it was two o'clock and Ralph was sound asleep on the floor. My mother told me to put him up on Fudge's new bed while she took the rest of the children back to the living room.

I tried and tried but I couldn't lift Ralph. He must weigh a ton. So I left him sleeping on Fudge's floor and closed the door so he wouldn't hear any noise. On my way back to the living room I wished the others would fall asleep too.

'Peter,' my mother suggested, 'why don't you show

them Dribble?'

'Mom! Dribble's my pet.' You don't go around using a pet to entertain a bunch of little kids. Didn't my mother know that?

'Please, Peter,' my mother said. 'We've still got half an hour left and I don't know what to do with them any more.'

'Dribble!' Fudge hollered. 'Dribble . . . Dribble . . . Dribble!'

I guess Sam and Jennie liked the way that sounded because they started to shout, 'Dribble . . . Dribble . . . Dribble!' even though they didn't know what they were talking about.

'Oh . . . all right,' I said. 'I'll show you Dribble. But you've got to promise to be very quiet. You mustn't make a sound. You might scare him . . . okay?'

They all said 'Okay.' My mother went into the kitchen to chat with Grandma and Mrs. Rudder. I went into my room and came back carrying Dribble in his bowl. I put my finger over my lips to remind Fudge and his friends to be quiet. It worked. At first nobody said a word.

I put Dribble down on a table. Fudge and Sam and Jennie stood over his bowl.

'Oh . . . turtle!' Jennie said.

'Yes, Dribble's a turtle. *My* turtle,' I said in a soft voice.

'See . . . see,' Fudge whispered.

'They can all see,' I told Fudge.

'Nice turtle,' Sam said.

I wondered why he wasn't afraid this time.

'What does Dribble do?' Jennie asked.

'Do? He doesn't do anything special,' I said. 'He's a turtle. He does turtle things.'

'Like what?' Jennie asked.

What was with this kid, anyway? 'Well,' I said, 'he swims around a little and he sleeps on his rock and he eats.'

'Does he make?' Jennie asked.

'Make?' I said.

'Make a tinkle?'

'Oh, that. Well, sure. I guess so.'

Jennie laughed. So did Sam and Fudge.

'I make tinkles too. Want to see?' Jennie asked.

'No,' I said.

'See . . . see,' Fudge laughed, pointing at Jennie.

Jennie had a big smile on her face. Next thing I knew there was a puddle on the rug.

'Mom!' I hollered. 'Come quick!'

My mother dashed in from the kitchen. 'What, Peter? What is it?'

'Just look at what Jennie did,' I said.

'What is that?' my mother asked, eyeing the puddle.

'She made on the floor,' I said. 'And on purpose!'

'Oh, Jennie!' my mother cried. 'You didn't!'

'Did too,' Jennie said.

'That was very naughty!' my mother told her. 'You come with me.' She scooped up Jennie and carried her into the bathroom.

After that Mom mopped up the puddle.

Finally the doorbell rang. It was two-thirty. The party was over. I could hardly believe it. I was beginning to think it would never end.

First Ralph's mother came. She had to wake him up to

get him out of the apartment. I guess even *she* couldn't carry him.

Next Jennie's mother came. Mom gave her Jennie's wet pants in a Baggie. That was all she had to do. Jennie's mother was plenty embarrassed.

Sam's mother came last. But he didn't want to go home. Now that he was used to us I guess he liked us. He cried, 'More party . . . MORE!'

'Another time,' his mother said, dragging him out of our apartment by the arm.

My mother flopped down in a chair. Grandma brought her two aspirins and a glass of water. 'Here, dear,' she said. 'Maybe these will help.'

My mother swallowed the pills. She held her head.

'Three is kind of young for a party,' I told my mother.

'Peter Warren Hatcher . . .' my mother began.

'Yes?' I asked.

'You are absolutely right!'

I flopped down next to my mother. She put her arm around me. Then we watched Fudge work his new jack-in-the-box.

Later, when my father came home, he said, 'How did Fudge's party go?'

My mother and I looked at each other and we laughed.

– 6 –
Fang Hits Town

Fudge liked his new bed a lot. There was just one problem. He fell out of it every night. By the fourth night my mother and father got smart. They pushed the bed against the wall and surrounded the other side with chairs. Now there was no place for Fudge to fall.

But every morning my mother found him curled up in one of the chairs. My father said they could have saved their money, since Fudge was so happy sleeping in an old chair!

On Saturday we had to go to the dentist. He wanted to check Fudge's mouth again. To make sure everything healed all right since his flying experience. Dr. Brown is an old friend of my father's. They went to school together. He's always saying he takes special good care of me and Fudge because we're chips off the old block (the old block being my father). His office is on the other side of the park. It's near Madison Avenue. My mother said we'd make a day of it. And wouldn't that be fun!

'I'd rather go to the movies with Jimmy Fargo,' I told her.

'But we'll have such a good time,' my mother said. 'The three of us will go out for lunch and then we'll get new shoes for you and Fudge.'

'I've been out to lunch with Fudge,' I reminded her.

'He's growing up, Peter. He knows how to behave now.'

'I'd still rather go to the movies with Jimmy.'

'Well, you're coming with me. And that's that!'

I wasn't looking forward to my day. And Saturday is always the best day of the week. Every Saturday morning I clean out Dribble's bowl. Sometimes, if Fudge is very good, I let him watch. I do it in the bathroom. First I take Dribble out of his bowl and let him crawl around in the bath. I'm afraid to put him down on the floor – somebody might step on him. But in the bath I know he's safe.

Next, I take the rocks out of his bowl and wash them. The last thing I do is wash the bowl itself. I really scrub it. I even rinse it two or three times to make sure all the soap is out. When I'm done with that I put the rocks back in and fill it with just the right amount of water. After I put Dribble back in his bowl I feed him. Usually he goes right to sleep on his favourite rock. I guess running around in the bath-tub really makes my turtle tired.

Today, I finished with Dribble just in time. My mother was rushing, mumbling about getting us to Dr. Brown's office in time for our appointment.

When we were outside we took the crosstown bus, then walked a few blocks to his office.

As soon as the nurse saw Fudge she said, 'How's my favourite patient?' She gave him a hug and a little book to read. To me she said, 'Good morning, Peter.'

It burns me up the way people treat Fudge. He's not so special. He's just little, that's all! But some day he's going to be nine years old too. I can't wait until he is. Then he'll know there's nothing so great about him after all.

Soon the nurse said, 'Fudge, Dr. Brown is ready for you. Come with me now.' Fudge took the nurse's hand.

Dr. Brown has this rule about mothers in the examining room with kids – they're not allowed! Mothers are a big problem, Dr. Brown told me once. I agreed.

I looked through a *National Geographic* magazine while I waited. After a few minutes the nurse came out and whispered something to my mother. I looked up, wondering what the big secret was.

Then my mother said, 'Peter, Dr. Brown would like you to help him with Fudge.'

'Help him?' I said. 'I'm no dentist!'

The nurse said, 'Peter, dear . . . if you'll just come with me I'm sure everything will work out fine.'

So I went with the nurse. 'What do I have to do?' I asked her.

'Oh, not much. Dr. Brown just wants you to show Fudge how you open your mouth and how he checks your teeth.'

'What do I have to do that for?' I asked. 'I don't need a checkup yet. I just had one last month.'

'Your brother won't open his mouth this morning,' the nurse whispered.

'He won't?' I whispered back.

'No, he won't!' she said again.

I thought that was pretty funny. I never considered refusing to open my mouth at the dentist's office. When he says 'Open' – I open!

When we reached the examining room Fudge was sitting in the big chair. He had a towel around his neck and he looked all ready for action.

Dr. Brown was showing him lots of little things and explaining what he does with each one. Fudge kept nodding but he wouldn't open his mouth.

'Ah . . . Peter!' Dr. Brown said when he saw me. 'Would you open your mouth so I can count your teeth?'

That's what he tells little kids he's doing – counting their teeth. Little kids will believe anything!

I went along with Dr. Brown's joke. I opened my mouth very wide. Much wider than when I'm the real patient. He put his mirror in and said, 'Wonderful teeth. Just beautiful. A regular chip off the old block! Such a shame your brother can't open his mouth the way you do.'

'Can so,' Fudge said.

'No,' Dr. Brown told him, 'you can't open your mouth nearly as good as Peter.'

'Can so . . . see!' Fudge opened his mouth.

'No, I'm sorry, Fudge,' Dr. Brown said, 'it's still not as good as Peter.'

So Fudge opened his mouth really wide. 'Count teeth!' he said. 'Count Fudgie's teeth!'

'Well . . .' Dr. Brown pretended to think about it.

'COUNT!' Fudge shouted.

'Well . . .' Dr. Brown said again, scratching his head. 'I guess as long as you're here I might as well count your teeth.' So he checked Fudge's mouth.

When he was through Fudge said, 'See . . . see . . . just like Pee-tah!'

'Yes,' Dr. Brown said, smiling. 'I can see that. You're just like Peter.' He gave me a wink.

I liked the way Dr. Brown tricked Fudge into opening his mouth. So when he was through examining him I whispered, 'Couldn't you make Fudge some false teeth . . . until his grown-up ones come in?'

'No. He'll just have to wait,' Dr. Brown said.

'But he looks like he has fangs,' I told him.

'You'd better not say that in front of your mother,' Dr. Brown said.

'I know it. She's not too big on fangs!'

Dr. Brown thanked me for helping him. My mother made another appointment for Fudge. The nurse kissed my brother good-bye and we left.

'That wasn't so bad, was it, Peter?' my mother said.

'It could have been worse,' I admitted.

We headed for Bloomingdale's, where we get our shoes. There are five salesmen in the children's shoe department. Two of them my mother doesn't like. She thinks they don't measure my feet carefully. That all they care about is selling shoes, even if they don't have the right sizes in stock. The other ones my mother thinks are okay. There's one she likes a lot. His name is Mr. Berman. I like him too – because he's funny. He usually makes believe that the right shoe goes on the left foot or that Fudge's shoes are really for me. Anyway, when Mr. Berman waits on us, buying shoes is almost fun.

Today Mr. Berman spotted us right away. He always remembers our name. 'Well, if it isn't the Hatcher boys,' he said.

'In the flesh,' I told him.

Fudge opened his mouth for Mr. Berman. 'See . . . see . . . all gone!'

'His teeth,' my mother explained to Mr. Berman. 'He knocked out his top two front teeth.'

'Well, congratulations!' Mr. Berman said. 'That calls for a celebration.' He reached into his jacket pocket and pulled out two lollipops. He handed one to me and one to Fudge.

'Ohhh,' Fudge said. 'Lolly!'

Mine was root-beer flavoured. I hate root beer. But I thanked Mr. Berman anyway. 'I'll save it for after lunch,' I told him, handing it to my mother. She put it into her purse. Fudge got a lemon lolly. He ripped off the paper and started sucking right away.

'Now then . . . what'll it be, boys?' Mr. Berman asked.

My mother answered. 'Brown-and-white saddles for Fudge and loafers for Peter.'

'Okay, Peter . . . let's see how those feet have grown.'

I slipped out of my old shoes and stood up. I stuck my left foot into Mr. Berman's foot measure. Then he turned it around and I put my right foot in. That's another reason why my mother thinks Mr. Berman is good at selling shoes. He measures both feet. Some other salesmen only measure one. My mother says feet can be different sizes, even on the same person. And it's important to make sure the size fits the biggest foot.

'What colour loafers, Peter?' Mr. Berman asked.

'Brown,' I said. 'Same as my old ones.'

When Mr. Berman went into the back to look for shoes for me my mother noticed the hole in the toe of my sock.

'Oh, Peter! Why didn't you tell me you had a hole in your sock?'

'I didn't know I had one,' I said.

'Oh . . . I'm so embarrassed!'

'It's my sock, Mom. Why should you be embarrassed?' I asked.

'Well, it looks terrible. I mean, to come shopping for shoes with a hole in your sock! That's just awful. Can't you hide it a little?'

'Where should I hide it?'

'Try to get the hole in between your toes, so it doesn't show,' my mother said.

I wiggled my sock around trying to rearrange my hole. My mother sure worries about silly things!

Mr. Berman came out with pairs of loafers. He likes to try different sizes to make sure I'm getting the right one. One pair was much too big. The other pair fit fine.

'Wear or wrap?' Mr. Berman asked my mother.

'Wrap, please,' she said. 'We'll wear the old ones home.'

I have never been allowed to wear new shoes home from the store. Don't ask me why. But my mother always has the new pair wrapped up and I can't wear them until the next day.

When I was finished Mr. Berman untied Fudge's shoes and measured his feet.

'Brown-and-white saddle shoes,' my mother reminded him.

Mr. Berman went into the back and returned with two shoe boxes. But when he opened the first box and Fudge saw the saddle shoes he said, 'No!'

'No what?' my mother asked him.

'No shoes!' Fudge said. He started kicking his feet.

'Don't be silly, Fudgie! You need new shoes,' my mother told him.

'NO! NO! NO!' he hollered. Everybody in the shoe department looked over at us.

'Here's the perfect size,' Mr. Berman told Fudge, holding up one shoe. 'Wait till you see how nice these new shoes will feel.'

Fudge kicked some more. It was impossible for Mr.

Berman to get the shoes on his feet. He screamed, '*No shoes*! NO! NO! NO!'

My mother grabbed hold of him but he was wiggling all around. He managed to give Mr. Berman a kick in the face. Lucky for him Fudge only had on socks.

'Now look, Fudge,' my mother said, 'you must get new shoes. Your old ones are too small. So what kind do you want?'

I don't know why my mother bothered to talk to him like he was a regular person. Because when Fudge gets himself into a temper tantrum he doesn't listen to anything. By that time he had thrown himself onto the floor where he beat his fists against the rug.

'What kind do you want, Fudge? Because we're not leaving here until you have new shoes!' my mother said, like she meant it.

I figured we'd be there for the rest of the day . . . or maybe the week! How could my mother have been embarrassed over a little hole in my sock and then act like nothing much was happening when her other son was on the floor yelling and screaming and carrying on!

'I'm going to count to three,' my mother told Fudge. 'And then I want you to tell me which shoes you want. Ready? One . . . two . . . three . . .'

Fudge sat up. 'Like Pee-tah's!' he said.

I smiled. I guess the kid really looks up to me. He even wants to wear the same kind of shoes. But everybody knows you can't buy loafers for such a little guy.

'They don't come in your size,' Mr. Berman told Fudge.

'YES! YES! YES! LIKE PEE-TAH'S!' Fudge hollered.

Mr. Berman held up his hands and looked at my mother, as if to say, *I give up*.

But my mother said, 'I have an idea.' She motioned for me and Mr. Berman to come closer.

I had the feeling I wasn't going to like her idea. But I listened anyway. 'I think we'll have to play a little joke on Fudge,' she said.

'What do you mean?' I asked.

'Well . . . suppose Mr. Berman brings out a pair of saddle shoes in your size and . . .'

'Oh no!' I said. 'You're not going to get me to wear saddle shoes. Never!'

'Let me finish,' my mother said. 'Mr. Berman can bring them out and you can try them on and then Fudge will think that's what you're getting. But when we leave we'll take the loafers.'

'That's mean,' I said. 'You're taking advantage of him.'

'Since when do you worry about that?' my mother asked.

'Since now,' I told her.

'Look, Peter,' my mother said, checking her watch, 'it's twelve o'clock. I'm starved.'

'Me too,' I said.

'Well then, if you ever want to get some lunch let's try my idea.'

'Okay . . . okay,' I said.

I sat back in my chair while Mr. Berman hurried to the stockroom again.

Fudge looked up at me from his position on the floor. 'Like Pee-tah's!' he said.

'Yeah . . . sure, Fudge,' I told him.

Mr. Berman came back with a pair of brown-and-white saddle shoes in my size. I tried them on. Did they look ugly!

'See Peter's nice saddle shoes,' my mother said. 'Now Fudgie tries on his nice saddle shoes.'

Fudge let Mr. Berman get him into his new pair of shoes.

'See,' he said. 'See . . . like Pee-tah's.' He held up a foot.

'That's right, Fudge,' I said. 'Just like mine.' You sure can fool little kids easy!

'Wear or wrap?' Mr. Berman asked my mother, while Fudge walked around in his new shoes.

'Wrap, of course!' she said.

I wondered what my mother would tell Fudge tomorrow when I wore my new loafers. Oh well, that really wasn't my worry. It was her idea!

When Fudge was back in his old shoes and our package was ready, Mr. Berman gave my brother a striped balloon. He offered one to me too. I refused. How could he think a person in fourth grade might want a shoe store balloon?

'That wasn't so terrible, was it, Peter?' my mother said, as we left the store.

'It wasn't?' I asked.

'Well, it could have been worse!' my mother said.

'I suppose,' I answered.

We went to Hamburger Heaven for lunch. We sat in a booth. Fudge tossed his balloon around while my mother ordered for him and then for herself. I ordered my own lunch – a hamburger with everything on it and a chocolate milk shake. Fudge was getting a kiddie special, meaning a hamburger without the roll, some mashed potatoes, and a side order of green peas.

When our lunch was served my mother cut Fudge's hamburger into tiny pieces which he shoved into his mouth with his fingers. Then she handed him a spoon and told him to eat his mashed potatoes. But instead of eating them he smeared them on the wall. 'See,' he said.

'I thought you told me he wouldn't behave like that any more!' I said to my mother.

'Fudgie! That's naughty. You stop it right now!' my mother said.

But Fudge sang, 'Eat it or wear it!' and he dumped the whole dish of peas over his head.

I laughed. I couldn't help it. He looked so silly with the peas falling from his hair. And when I eat and laugh at the same time I choke. So I choked on my pickle and my mother had to whack me on the back, which gave Fudge another chance to spread mashed potatoes on the wall.

That's when the waitress asked my mother did we want anything else.

'No thank you,' my mother said. 'We have more than enough now!' She wiped the wall with her napkin and told Fudge he was very, very naughty.

'Not me,' Fudge said. 'Not me!'

'Yes, you!' my mother told him. 'Why can't you eat like Peter? See how nice Peter eats?'

Fudge didn't say anything. He just stuck his fork into his balloon. It popped and he screamed. 'All gone! Want more balloon! MORE.'

'Shut up!' I told him. 'Can't you ever act human?'

'That's enough, Peter!' my mother said.

She should have slugged him. That would teach that brother of mine how to behave in Hamburger Heaven!

We took a cab home. Fudge fell asleep on the way. He had his fingers in his mouth and made his slurping noise. My mother whispered to me, 'Our day wasn't *that* bad, was it, Peter?' I didn't answer. I just looked out of the taxi window and decided that I would never spend a day with Farley Drexel Hatcher again.

7

The Flying Train Committee

In January our class started a project on The City. Mrs. Haver, our teacher, divided us up into committees by where we live. That way we could work at home. My committee was me, Jimmy Fargo, and Sheila. Our topic was Transportation. We decided to make my apartment the meeting place because I'm the only one of the three of us who's got his own bedroom. In a few weeks each committee has to hand in a booklet, a poster, and be ready to give an oral report.

The first day we got together after school we bought a yellow posterboard. Jimmy wanted a blue one but Sheila talked him out of it. 'Yellow is a much brighter colour,' she explained. 'Everything will show up on it. Blue is too dull.'

Sheila thinks she's smarter than me and Jimmy put together – just because she's a girl! So right away she told us she would be in charge of our booklet and me and Jimmy could do most of the poster. As long as we check with her first, to make sure she likes our ideas. We agreed, since Sheila promised to do ten pages of written work and we would only do five.

After we bought the yellow posterboard we went to the library. We took out seven books on transportation. We wanted to learn all we could about speed, traffic congestion, and pollution. We arranged to meet on Tuesday and Thursday afternoons for the next two weeks.

Our first few committee meetings turned out like this: We got to my place by three-thirty, had a snack, then played with Dribble for another half hour. Sheila gave up on cooties when Fudge lost his front teeth. But it still isn't much fun to have her hanging around. She's always complaining that she got stuck with the worst possible committee. And that me and Jimmy fool more than we work. We only put up with her because we have no choice!

Sheila and Jimmy have to be home for supper before five-thirty. So at five o'clock we start cleaning up. We keep our equipment under my bed in a shoe box. We have a set of Magic Markers, Elmer's glue, Scotch tape, a really sharp pair of scissors, and a container of silver sparkle.

Sheila carries our committee booklet back and forth with her. She doesn't trust us enough to leave it at my house! The posterboard fits under my bed, along with our supplies. We stack the library books on my desk. The reason I make sure we clean up good is that my mother told me if I left a mess we'd have to find some place else to work.

By our third meeting I told Jimmy and Sheila that I'd figured out the solution to New York City's traffic problems. 'We have to get rid of the traffic,' I said. 'There shouldn't be any cars or buses or taxis allowed in the city. What we really need is a citywide monorail system.'

'That's too expensive,' Sheila said. 'It sounds good but it's not practical.'

'I disagree!' I told Sheila. 'It's very practical. Besides getting rid of traffic it'll get rid of air pollution and it'll get people where they're going a lot faster.'

'But it's not practical, Peter!' Sheila said again. 'It costs too much.'

I opened one of my books on transportation and read Sheila a quote. '"A monorail system is the hope of the future".' I cleared my throat and looked up.

'But we can't write a report just about the monorail,' Sheila said. 'We'll never be able to fill twenty written pages with that.'

'We can write big,' Jimmy suggested.

'No!' Sheila said. 'I want a good mark on this project. Peter, you can write your five pages about the monorail system and how it works. Jimmy, you can write your five pages about pollution caused by transportation. And I'll write ten pages on the history of transportation in the city.' Sheila folded her arms and smiled.

'Can I write big?' Jimmy asked.

'I don't care how big you write as long as you put your name on your five pages!' Sheila told him.

'That's not fair!' Jimmy said. 'This is supposed to be a group project. Why should I have to put my name on my five pages?'

'Then don't write BIG!' Sheila shouted.

'Okay. Okay . . . I'll write so small Mrs. Haver will need a microscope to see the letters.'

'Very funny,' Sheila said.

'Look,' I told both of them, 'I think all our written work should be in the same handwriting. That's the only fair way. Otherwise Mrs. Haver will know who did what. And it won't be a group project.'

'Say, that's a good idea,' Jimmy said. 'Which one of us has the best handwriting?'

Me and Jimmy looked at Sheila.

'Well, I do have a nice even script,' Sheila said. 'But if I'm going to copy over your written work you better give it to me by next Tuesday. Otherwise, I won't have enough time to do the job. And you two better get going on your poster.' Sheila talked like she was the teacher and we were the kids.

Me and Jimmy designed the whole poster ourselves. We used the pros and cons of each kind of transportation. It was really clever. We divided a chart into land, sea, and air and we planned an illustration for each – with the aeroplane done in silver sparkle and the letters done in red and blue Magic Marker. We got halfway through the lettering that day. We also sketched in the ship, the plane, and the truck.

When Sheila saw it she asked, 'Is that supposed to be a train?'

'No,' I told her. 'It's a truck.'

'It doesn't look like one,' she said.

'It will,' Jimmy told her, 'when it's finished.'

'I hope so,' Sheila said. 'Because right now it looks like a flying train!'

'That's because the ground's not under it yet,' Jimmy said.

'Yeah,' I agreed. 'See, we've got to make it look like it's on a street. Right now it does kind of look like it's up in space.'

'So does the ship,' Sheila said.

'We'll put some water lines around it,' I told her.

'And some clouds around the plane,' Sheila said.

'Listen,' Jimmy hollered, 'did anybody ever tell you you're too bossy? This poster is ours! You do the booklet. Remember . . . that's the way you wanted it!'

'See . . . there you go again!' Sheila said. 'You keep forgetting this is a committee. We're supposed to work together.'

'Working together doesn't mean you give the orders and we carry them out,' Jimmy said.

My feelings exactly! I thought.

Sheila didn't answer Jimmy. She picked up her things, got her coat, and left.

'I hope she never comes back,' Jimmy said.

'She'll be back,' I told him. 'We're her committee.'

Jimmy laughed. 'Yeah . . . we're all one happy committee!'

I put our poster under the bed, said good-bye to Jimmy, then washed up for supper.

My mother was being pretty nice about our committee meetings. She arranged to have Fudge play at Ralph's apartment on Tuesdays and at Jennie's on Thursdays. Sam has the chickenpox, so he can't play at all.

I was glad that next week would be our last committee meeting after school. I was sick of Sheila and I was getting sick of Transportation. Besides, now that I knew a monorail system was the only way to save our city I was getting upset that the mayor and all the other guys that run things at City Hall weren't doing anything about installing one. If *I* know that's the best method of city transportation how come *they* don't know it?

The next day when I came home from school I went into my bedroom to see Dribble like I always do. Fudge was in there, sitting on my bed.

'Why are you in my room?' I asked him.

He smiled.

'You know you're not supposed to be in here. This is *my* room.'

'Want to see?' Fudge said.

'See what?'

'Want to see?'

'What? What are you talking about?' I asked.

He jumped off my bed and crawled underneath it. He came out with our poster. He held it up. 'See,' he said. 'Pretty!'

'What did you do?' I yelled. 'What did you do to our poster?' It was covered all over with scribbles in every colour Magic Marker. It was ruined! *It was a mess and it was ruined.* I was ready to kill Fudge. I grabbed my poster and ran into the kitchen to show it to my mother. I could hardly speak. 'Look,' I said, feeling a lump in my throat. 'Just look at what he did to my poster.' I felt tears come to my eyes but I didn't care. 'How could you let him?' I asked my mother. 'How? Don't you care about me?'

I threw the poster down and ran into my room. I slammed the door, took off my shoe, and flung it at the wall. It made a black mark where it hit. Well, so what!

Soon I heard my mother hollering – and then, Fudge crying. After a while my mother knocked on my bedroom door and called, 'Peter, may I come in?'

I didn't answer.

She opened the door and walked over to my bed. She sat down next to me. 'I'm very sorry,' she said.

I still didn't say anything.

'Peter,' she began.

I didn't look at her.

She touched my arm. 'Peter . . . please listen . . .'

'Don't you see, Mom? I can't even do my homework without him messing it up. It just isn't fair! I wish he was never born. *Never!* I hate him!'

'You don't hate him,' my mother said. 'You just think you do.'

'Don't tell me,' I said. 'I mean it. I really can't stand that kid!'

'You're angry,' my mother told me. 'I know that and I don't blame you. Fudge had no right to touch your poster. I spanked him.'

'You did?' I asked. Fudge never gets spanked. My parents don't believe in spanking. 'You really spanked him?' I asked again.

'Yes,' my mother said.

'Hard?' I asked.

'On his backside,' she told me.

I thought that over.

'Peter . . .' My mother put her arm around me. 'I'll buy you a new posterboard tomorrow. It was really my fault. I should never have let him into your room.'

'That's why I need a lock on my door,' I said.

'I don't like locks on doors. We're a family. We don't have to lock each other out.'

'If I had a lock Fudge wouldn't have found my poster!'

'It won't happen again,' my mother promised.

I wanted to believe her, but really I didn't. Unless she tied him up I knew my brother would get into my room again.

The next day, while I was at school, my mother bought a new yellow posterboard. The hard part was explaining to Jimmy that we had to start all over again. He was a good sport about it. He said this time he'd make sure his truck didn't look like a flying train. And I said, this time I'd make pencil marks first so my letters didn't go uphill.

Our committee met that afternoon. Sheila didn't mention the last time. Neither did we. Me and Jimmy worked on the poster while Sheila copied our written work into the booklet. We'd be ready to give our oral report to the class on Monday. Not like some committees who hadn't even started yet!

By five o'clock we had finished our poster and Sheila was almost done with the cover for our booklet. Jimmy walked over and stood behind her, watching her work.

After a minute he yelled, 'What do you think you're doing, Sheila?'

I got up from the floor and joined them at my desk. I took a look at the cover. It was pretty nice. It said:

TRANSPORTATION IN THE CITY

Under that it said:

BY SHEILA TUBMAN, PETER HATCHER,
AND JAMES FARGO

And under that in small letters it said:

handwritten by miss sheila tubman

Now I knew why Jimmy was mad. 'Oh no!' I said, holding my hand to my head. 'How could you!'

Sheila didn't say anything.

'It's not fair,' I told her. 'We didn't put our names on the poster!'

'But the cover's all done,' Sheila said. 'Can't you see that? I'll never get the letters so straight again. It looks perfect!'

'Oh no!' Jimmy shouted. 'We're not handing the booklet in like that. I'll rip it up before I let you!' He grabbed the booklet and threatened to tear it in half.

Sheila screamed. 'You wouldn't! I'll kill you! Give it back to me, Jimmy Fargo!' She was ready to cry.

I knew Jimmy wouldn't tear it up but I didn't say so. 'Peter . . . make him give it back!'

'Will you take off that line about your handwriting?' I asked.

'I can't. It'll ruin the booklet.'

'Then I think he should rip it up,' I said.

Sheila stamped her foot. 'Ooooh! I hate you both!'

'You don't really,' I told her. 'You just think you do.'

'I know I do!' Sheila cried.

'That's because you're angry right now,' I said. I couldn't help smiling.

Sheila jumped up and tried to get the booklet but Jimmy held it over his head and he's much taller than Sheila. She had no chance at all.

Finally she sat down and whispered, 'I give up. You win. I'll take my name off.'

'You promise?' Jimmy asked.

'I promise,' Sheila said.

Jimmy set the booklet down on my desk in front of Sheila. 'Okay,' he said. 'Start.'

'I'm not going to make a whole new cover,' Sheila said. 'What I'll do is turn this bottom line into a decoration.' She picked up a Magic Marker and made little flowers out of the words. Soon, *handwritten by miss sheila tubman,* turned into sixteen small flowers. 'There,' Sheila said. 'It's done.'

'It looks pretty good,' I told her.

'It would have looked better without those flowers,' Jimmy said. 'But at least it's fair now.'

That night I showed my mother and father our new poster. They thought it was great. Especially our silver-sparkle aeroplane. My mother put the poster on top of the refrigerator so it would be safe until the next day, when I would take it to school.

Now I had nothing to worry about. Sheila had the booklet, the poster was safe, and our committee was finished before schedule. I went into my room to relax. Fudge was sitting on the floor, near my bed. My shoe-box of supplies was in front of him. His face was a mess of Magic Marker colours and he was using my extra sharp scissors to snip away at his hair. And the hair he snipped was dropping into Dribble's bowl – which he had in front of him on the floor!

'See,' he said. 'See Fudge. Fudgie's a barber!'

That night I found out hair doesn't hurt my turtle. I picked off every strand from his shell. I cleaned out his bowl and washed off his rocks. He seemed happy.

Two things happened the next day. One was my mother had to take Fudge to the real barber to do something about his hair. He had plenty left at the back, but just about nothing in front and on top. The barber said there wasn't much he could do until the hair grew back. Between his fangs and his hair he was getting funnier-looking every day.

The second was my father came home with a chain latch for my bedroom door. I could reach it when I stood on tip-toe, but that brother of mine couldn't reach it at all – no matter what!

Our committee was the first to give its report. Mrs. Haver said we did a super job. She liked our poster a lot. She thought the silver-sparkle aeroplane was the best. The only thing she asked us was, how come we included a picture of a flying train?

8

The TV Star

Aunt Linda is my mother's sister. She lives in Boston. Last week she had a baby girl. So now I have a new cousin. My mother decided to fly to Boston to see Aunt Linda and the new baby.

'I'll only be gone for the weekend,' my mother told me.

I was sitting on her bed watching her pack. 'I know,' I said.

'Daddy will take care of you and Fudge.'

'I know,' I said again.

'Are you sure you'll be all right?' she asked me.

'Sure. Why not?'

'Will you help Daddy with Fudge?'

'Sure, Mom. Don't worry.'

'I'm not worrying. It's just that Daddy is so . . . well, you know . . . he doesn't know much about taking care of children.' Then she closed her suitcase.

'We'll be fine, Mom,' I said. I was really looking forward to the weekend. My father doesn't care about keeping things neat. He never examines me to see if I'm clean. And he lets me stay up late at night.

On Friday morning all four of us rode down in the elevator to say good-bye to my mother.

Henry looked at the suitcase. 'You going away, Mr. Hatcher?' he asked.

My mother answered. 'No, I am, Henry. My sister

just had her first baby. I'm flying to Boston for the week-end . . . to help out.'

'New baby,' Fudge said. 'Baby baby baby.'

Nobody paid any attention to him. Sometimes my brother just talks to hear the sound of his own voice.

'Have a nice visit, Mrs. Hatcher,' Henry told my mother when we reached the lobby.

'Thank you, Henry,' my mother said. 'Keep an eye on my family for me.'

'Will do, Mrs. Hatcher,' Henry said, giving my father a wink.

Outside my father hailed a taxi. He put the suitcase in first, then held the door for my mother. When she was settled in the cab my father said, 'Don't worry about us. We'll be just fine.'

'Just fine . . . just fine, Mommy,' Fudge yelled.

'Bye, Mom. See you Sunday,' I said.

My mother blew us kisses. Then her cab drove away.

My father sighed while Fudge jumped up and down calling, 'Bye, Mommy . . . bye bye bye!'

I had no school that day. The teachers were at a special meeting. So my father said he'd take me and Fudge to the office with him.

My father's office is in a huge building made of almost all glass. It's really a busy place. You never see people just sitting quietly at desks. Everyone's always rushing around. A person could get lost in there. My father has a private office and his own secretary. Her name is Janet and she's very pretty. I especially like her hair. It's thick and black. She has the longest eyelashes I've ever seen. Once I heard my mother say, 'Janet must have to get up at the crack of dawn to put on her face.'

My father just laughed when my mother said it.

Janet's seen me before but this was her first meeting with Fudge. I was glad his hair was finally growing back. I explained right off about his teeth. 'He'll look a lot better when he's older,' I said. 'He knocked out his front two, but when he's six or seven he'll get new ones.'

'See,' Fudge said, opening his mouth. 'All gone.'

My father said, 'Janet, the boys are going to be here for the morning. Can you amuse them while I clear up some work?'

'Certainly, Mr. Hatcher,' Janet said. 'You go ahead into your office and I'll take the boys on a tour of the rest of the agency.'

As soon as my father went into his private office Janet took out her handbag. She reached in and came up with a hairbrush, some lipstick, and a bag of crackers. 'Want some?' she asked me and Fudge.

'Okay,' I said, taking a handful. Fudge did the same. The crackers were shaped like little goldfish. I nibbled while Janet fixed herself up. She had a big folding mirror in her desk drawer. She set it on top of her desk and went to work on herself. When she was finished she looked exactly the same as when we came in. But I guess she didn't think so because she said, 'That's much better.' Then she put all her stuff away and took me by one hand and Fudge by the other.

We walked down a long hall through a doorway and into another section of the agency. We came to a room where there were a bunch of kids with mothers. I guess there were at least fifty of them. Most of the kids were kind of small, like Fudge. Some were crying.

'Is this a nursery school or what?' I asked Janet.

She laughed. 'They're here to try out for the new Toddle-Bike commercial.'

'You mean they all want to be the kid who rides the Toddle-Bike on TV?'

'Yes. At least their mothers want them to be picked,' Janet said. 'But we can only use one.'

'You mean only one out of all these kids is going to be picked?'

'That's right,' Janet said.

'Who picks him?' I asked.

'Your father and Mr. Denberg are doing it. But of course Mr. Vincent, the president of the Toddle-Bike company, has to approve.'

Just then a door opened and a secretary came out. 'Next,' she called to the waiting kids.

'My Murray's next!' a mother said.

'Oh no he's not!' another mother called. 'Sally is next.'

'Ladies . . . please! You'll all have a turn,' the secretary said.

Murray got to be next. He was a little redheaded kid. He wasn't in the other room for two minutes when the door opened and a big man with a cigar in his mouth came out. 'No, no, no!' he shouted. 'He's not the type at all.'

Murray was crying. His mother yelled at the big man. 'What do you know, anyway? You wouldn't know a treasure if you found one!' She shook her fist at him.

Janet whispered to me. 'That's Mr. Vincent, the president of Toddle-Bike.'

Mr. Vincent walked to the centre of the room. He

looked around at all the kids. When he looked over at us he pointed and called, 'There he is! That's the kid I want!'

I thought he meant me. I got excited. I could just see myself on TV riding the Toddle-Bike. All my friends would turn on their sets and say, 'Hey, look! There's Peter.'

While I was thinking about what fun it would be Mr. Vincent came over to us and grabbed Fudge. He lifted him up. 'Perfect!' he cried. 'He's perfect.'

The mothers who were waiting packed up their kids and left right away.

Mr. Vincent took off with Fudge in his arms. Janet chased him. She called, 'But, Mr. Vincent . . . you don't understand . . .'

I ran after Janet.

Mr. Vincent carried Fudge into the other room. He announced, 'I found him myself! The perfect kid to ride the Toddle-Bike in my new commercial.'

Mr. Vincent put Fudge down and took the cigar out of his mouth. There were two other men in the room. One of them was Mr. Denberg. The other one was my father.

'Hi, Daddy,' Fudge said.

'George,' my father told Mr. Vincent, 'this is my son! He's no actor or model. He can't make your Toddle-Bike commercial.'

'He doesn't have to be an actor or a model. He's perfect the way he is!' Mr. Vincent insisted.

'Now look, George . . . we want to make the best possible commercial for your company. But Fudge can't be the boy to ride the Toddle-Bike.'

'Now you listen, Hatcher!' Mr. Vincent raised his voice.

I wondered why he called my father Hatcher – just like Mr. Yarby did.

Mr. Vincent pointed to Fudge. 'Either that kid rides my Toddle-Bike or I take my account to another advertising agency. It's that simple.'

My father looked at Mr. Denberg.

'It's your decision, Warren,' Mr. Denberg told my father. 'I don't want to be the one to tell you what to do.'

My father picked up Fudge and held him on his lap. 'Would you like to ride the Toddle-Bike, Fudge? It's just like the one you have at home.'

'Why are you asking him?' I said. 'What does he know about making commercials?'

My father acted like he'd forgotten I was even around. 'I'm thinking, Peter,' he said. 'Please be quiet.'

'Well, Hatcher,' Mr. Vincent said. 'What'll it be? This kid of yours or do I move to another agency?'

I remembered how my father lost the Juicy-O account because of Fudge. Now maybe he'd lose this one too. And I don't think he can afford that.

Finally my father said, 'All right, George. You can use him . . . on one condition, though.'

'What's that, Hatcher?' Mr. Vincent asked.

'The commercial has to be made this afternoon. After today my son Fudge won't be available.'

'That's fine with me, Hatcher,' Mr. Vincent said.

'Is he going to get paid?' I asked my father.

'I'll worry about that, Peter,' my father said. That probably meant *yes*. He'd be paid and have lots of money in the bank. I'd have nothing. And some day I'd have to borrow from him. No – wait a minute – never! I'll never borrow money from Fudge. I'll starve first! 'Can I at least watch when you make the commercial?' I asked.

'Certainly,' my father said. 'You can watch the whole thing.'

I turned to Mr. Denberg. 'Will Fudge be famous?' I asked.

'No, not famous . . . but a lot of people will think he looks familiar,' Mr. Denberg said.

I turned to Mr. Vincent. 'Do you know he has no front top teeth?'

'That's part of his charm,' Mr. Vincent said.

'And he cut off all his hair two months ago.'

'Well, he looks fine now,' Mr. Vincent said.

'And he can't even talk in long sentences yet,' I told everyone in the room.

'He doesn't have to say a word,' Mr. Vincent told me.

I couldn't think of any other reason why Mr. Vincent shouldn't use Fudge in his Toddle-Bike commercial. It was settled. Soon Fudge would be a famous television star and I would be plain old Peter Hatcher – fourth grade nothing.

'Let's begin right after lunch,' Mr. Denberg said. 'We should get it filmed in about two hours.'

While my father and Mr. Denberg worked out all the arrangements I asked Janet where the men's room was. She walked me to it. I told her thank you and that she didn't have to wait. I'd find my own way back.

When I was safely inside I looked at myself in the mirror. *I wish Fudge had never been born,* I thought. *Everything good always happens to him! If he had to be*

*born I wish he could be nine or ten – like me. Then Mr.
Vincent wouldn't want him to be the one to ride the
Toddle-Bike in his commercial.*

Janet sent down to the coffee shop for some sandwiches and drinks. After we ate we all walked to another
section of the agency where the cameras were set up. A
make-believe street scene was the background. The
Toddle-Bike was shiny red. My father told Fudge all he
had to do was ride it around. Fudge liked that. He
zoomed all over the place. 'Vroom-vroom-vroom,' he
called.

My father, Mr. Vincent, and Janet sat on folding
chairs and watched the action. I sat on the floor, at my
father's side. Mr. Denberg was the director. He said,
'Okay, Fudge . . . we're ready to begin now. You ride the
Toddle-Bike where I tell you to and I'll take a picture of
you doing it . . . all right?'

'No,' Fudge said.

'What does he mean, Hatcher?' Mr. Vincent asked.
'Why did he say *no*?'

My father groaned. 'Look, George . . . using Fudge
was your idea – not mine.'

Mr. Denberg tried again. 'Okay, Fudge . . . this is
it . . .'

The cameraman said, 'Start riding this way . . . ready,
set, go!'

Fudge sat there on the Toddle-Bike. But he wouldn't
pedal.

'Come on, kid . . . let's go!' the cameraman called.

'No. Don't want to!' Fudge answered.

'What's with this kid, Mr. Hatcher?' the cameraman
asked.

'Fudge,' my father said, 'do what the nice man tells you to.'

'No! Don't have to!'

Janet whispered to my father. 'How about some cookies, Mr. Hatcher?'

'Good idea, Janet,' my father told her.

'I have some Oreos right here,' she said, patting her handbag. 'Shall I give them to him?'

'One at a time,' my father said.

Janet walked across the room to Fudge. He was still sitting on the Toddle-Bike. 'If you do what the nice man says, you can have a cookie,' Janet told him.

'Show me,' Fudge said.

Janet held up a box of Oreos. *She was really well prepared*, I thought. *She must eat all day long, what with the crackers shaped like goldfish and a whole box of Oreos too*. I wondered what else she had in that handbag.

'Give me,' Fudge said.

Janet held up one cookie. Fudge reached for it, but Janet didn't let him get it. 'If you do what the nice man says you can have an Oreo. Maybe even two or three Oreos.'

'First cookie,' Fudge said.

'First do what the nice man says,' Janet told him.

'No! First cookie!'

'Give him one, Janet,' Mr. Denberg called. 'We haven't got all day to fool around.'

Janet gave Fudge one Oreo. He ate it up.

'Okay, kid . . . all ready now?' the cameraman said. 'You ride over to me.'

Fudge didn't do it.

Mr. Vincent was losing his patience. 'Hatcher,' he hollered. 'You get that son of yours to ride my Toddle-Bike or I'm taking my whole account away from you and your agency!'

'Must I remind you, George . . . using Fudge was your idea – not mine!' my father said.

'Forget about whose idea it was, Hatcher. He's your kid. You better get through to him . . . now!'

'I have an idea,' my father said. He walked to a corner of the room and beckoned to the others. Mr. Denberg and Mr. Vincent gathered around him, along with the cameraman and Janet. They looked like a bunch of football players huddled together talking about the next play.

Soon my father called me. 'Peter . . . would you join us, please?'

'Sure, Dad,' I said. 'What is it?'

'Peter . . . we want you to ride the Toddle-Bike for us. To show Fudge how it's done.'

'But he already knows how to ride,' I said. 'Didn't you see him zooming around?'

'He won't do it for the cameras, though,' my father explained. 'So we need your help.'

'Will I be in the commercial too?' I asked.

'Well, the Toddle-Bike is really for very young children,' Mr. Denberg said. 'Otherwise we'd have you do it in a minute.'

I got the message. It was like buying the shoes and like at Dr. Brown's office. They were going to use me to get Fudge to do what they wanted him to. I wondered how anybody would ever manage my brother without my help.

I walked over to Fudge and told him I was going to ride the Toddle-Bike. 'Get off,' I said.

Fudge held onto the bike. 'No . . . mine!'

'It's not yours,' my father told him.

But Fudge wouldn't move for anything. He closed his eyes and screamed. Can he scream loud when he tries!

So my father had to pull him off the Toddle-Bike. Fudge kicked and kept screaming and I'll bet Mr. Vincent was sorry that he ever spotted my brother in the first place.

I got on the Toddle-Bike. It was so small my knees practically touched the ground. But I managed to ride it around just where the cameraman told me to.

'See how nice Peter can ride the Toddle-Bike,' Janet said. 'Here, Peter . . . come have an Oreo. You did that so well you can have two or three if you want.'

Fudge stopped screaming. 'ME!' he said.

'What?' my father asked him.

'Me . . . ride . . . me!'

'You can't ride as well as Peter can,' Mr. Denberg said.

'Can so,' Fudge told him.

'I don't think so,' Mr. Denberg said. 'You already had a turn. You didn't do what I told you to do.'

'ME!'

'You want to try again?' my father asked.

'Again,' Fudge said. 'Again again again.'

'Well . . . I don't know,' Mr. Denberg said.

'Well . . .' Mr. Vincent said, chewing on his cigar.

'Well . . .' the cameraman said, scratching his head.

'Please!' Fudge begged.

I never heard my brother say *please* before.

Mr. Denberg said, 'Okay . . . we'll give you one more chance.'

Fudge ran to the Toddle-Bike. I got off and he jumped on. 'Now?' he asked Mr. Denberg.

'Now,' Mr. Denberg said. 'Ride this way, Fudge . . . over here . . . toward me.'

Fudge did as he was told. 'Just like Pee-tah!' he said. 'See . . . just like Pee-tah!'

Janet gave me a kiss on my cheek. 'You saved the day, Peter Hatcher!' she said.

When she wasn't looking I wiped my face. Her kiss was too juicy.

– 9 –
Just Another Rainy Day

The next day it rained. My father asked me how I'd like to go to the movies.

'Just me?' I asked.

'No. All three of us,' he said.

'Fudge is very young to go,' I said. 'Don't you think so?'

'Maybe. But I can't think of anything else to do with him. And that will take up a few hours.'

'You could give him some socks,' I suggested. 'You know how he loves to play with your socks.'

'Socks won't last the whole afternoon,' my father said. 'That's why I thought of the movies.'

'What'll we see, Dad?'

My father checked his *New York* magazine. '*A Bear's Life* is playing in the neighbourhood. How does that sound?'

'What's it about?' I asked.

'A bear's life, I guess,' my father said. 'It's rated G.'

I was thinking of a good Western with lots of action or else a picture rated R where you can't get in if you're under seventeen unless you're with your parents. But my father had made up his mind. *A Bear's Life* it was.

I suggested that my father get Fudge cleaned up. Because by then he was looking kind of messy. I don't think my father even put him into his pyjamas last night. He's been wearing the same polo shirt ever since my mother left yesterday morning.

By one o'clock we were ready to go. All three of us wore our raincoats and boots and my father took his big, black umbrella. One thing about New York – it's hard to get a cab when it's raining. But the movie theatre wasn't very far away. My father said the walk would do us all good. There were a lot of puddles. It was really pouring. I like to walk in the rain. Especially if it isn't too cold out. It feels nice when it wets your face.

I jumped over the puddles. My father avoided them too. But not Fudge. He jumped right into every one and splashed around like a little duck. By the time we got to the movie theatre the bottoms of his pants were soaked. My father took him into the men's room. He stuffed a bunch of paper towels up each pant leg so Fudge wouldn't have to sit around wet. At first Fudge complained. But when my father bought him a big box of popcorn he forgot about his stuffed pants.

Right after we got settled in our seats a big boy sat down in front of Fudge, so he had to change seats with my father. Now he was on the aisle, I was in the middle, and my father was on my other side.

When the lights dimmed Fudge said, 'Ohhh . . . dark.'

I told him, 'Be quiet. You can't talk in the movies.'

'Okay, Pee-tah,' he said.

That's when he started throwing his popcorn. At first I didn't notice but I wondered why the people in front of us were turning around every second. Then I heard Fudge whisper, 'Pow-pow-pow!' and I saw him throw a handful of popcorn.

I poked my father. 'He's throwing his popcorn,' I whispered.

My father reached across me and tapped Fudge on the leg. 'If you throw one more piece I'm going to take it away from you.'

'No throw!' Fudge said very loud.

'Shush . . .' the people in front of us said.

'Shush!' Fudge said back to them.

'You see,' I told my father, 'he's too young for the movies. He doesn't understand.'

But from the moment the first bear came on the screen Fudge sat still and watched. And after a while I forgot all about him and concentrated on the movie. It was much better than I thought it would be. It showed all these bear cubs and how they live.

I'm not sure when I realized Fudge was gone. I guess it was when I turned to ask him if he had any popcorn left. I had already finished mine and was still hungry. I was really surprised to see he wasn't there. I mean, one minute he was sitting right next to me and the next minute he was gone.

'Hey, Dad,' I whispered to my father. 'He's gone.'

'What?' my father said.

'Fudge isn't in his seat.'

My father looked over. 'Where did he go?'

'I don't know. I just noticed he was gone.'

'Let me out, Peter. I'll find him.'

'Should I come too?' I asked.

'No . . . you can sit here and watch the rest of the picture. He's probably wandering around by the candy counter.'

I stood up to let my father out. I wondered what my mother would think if she knew Fudge was lost in the movies.

A few minutes later the picture stopped – right in the middle of a scene. The sound track trailed off like a broken record. All the lights came on. The audience let out a groan. Some kids called, 'Boo . . . boo!'

Then my father and two ushers and a man in a suit came over to me. 'He was sitting right here,' my father told them, pointing to the empty seat on the aisle.

'Well,' the man in the suit said, 'we've checked the rest rooms and the office. He's not behind the candy counter. We'll have to search the theatre.' He cupped his hands around his mouth and shouted, 'Ladies and Gentlemen . . . may I have your attention please. We'll continue with our film in one moment. But first we have to find a three-year-old boy answering to the name of Fudge.'

Some people laughed when the man said his name. I guess *Fudge* does sound funny if you're not used to it. I thought, *Maybe he's been kidnapped! Would my mother be mad. That crazy kid! You can't even take him to the movies.* Then I thought, *Who'd want to kidnap him, anyway?*

'What should I do, Dad?' I said.

'Why don't you walk up and down this aisle and call him, Peter.'

'Okay,' I said.

'Here, Fudge,' I called, starting down my aisle. I sounded like I was calling a dog. 'Come on out, Fudge.'

When I got down to the first row and called, 'Here, Fudge,' he popped out at me. He scared me so bad I yelled, 'Ooooh . . .'

'Hi, Pee-tah,' he said.

'Hey . . . I found him,' I called. 'I found him . . . I found him . . . here he is!' Then I turned to my brother.

'You dope! What are you doing way down here? And why are you sitting on the floor?'

'Wanted to touch the bears,' Fudge said. 'But bears are all gone.' He spread out his arms and said, 'All gone' again.

My father and the ushers and the man in the suit ran to us. 'Fudge,' my father said, scooping him up. 'Are you all right?'

'He wanted to pet the bears,' I said. 'Can you beat that?'

'Well, I guess we can continue with the picture now,' the man in the suit said. He cupped his hands around his mouth again. 'Thank you, ladies and gentlemen. Our young man has been found safe and sound. Now we return to the conclusion of *A Bear's Life*.'

My father carried Fudge back to our seats. He held him on his lap for the rest of the show. I guess he wasn't taking any more chances!

Later, when we got home, my father explained to Fudge that movies are like TV. 'It's just a picture. There's nothing to touch.'

Fudge listened, but I don't know whether he believed my father. I had the feeling he still thought those bears were in the theatre somewhere. I made up my mind that I would never take my little brother to the movies. Never! At least not until he was nine or ten.

My father said he was going to cook us something special for dinner. To celebrate Finding Fudge in the Movies. I thought that was really strange. Because as far as I know my father can't cook anything. He doesn't even know where my mother keeps the peanut butter, the dishes, or the pots and pans. Lucky for him I was there to show him. 'What are you going to cook, Dad?'

'A super-duper omelette,' he said.

'Omelette? I'm not sure me and Fudge like omelettes.'

'You'll like this one,' my father said, humming as he gathered his ingredients together. 'Get me a big frying pan, Peter.'

'Okay,' I said. I gave it to him. He melted some butter in it.

'What's going in the super-duper omelette?' I asked while Fudge sat on the floor banging two pot covers together.

'Well, the eggs, of course,' my father said. 'Omelettes are made of eggs.'

'And what else?' I asked.

'Oh . . . I think I'll make a mushroom omelette.'

'Eggs and mushrooms?' I said.

'Yes, you'll love it!'

'I'm not so sure.'

'You'll see, Peter,' my father said.

I set up the table while my father cooked. I even put Fudge in his booster chair.

When the omelette was done my father brought it to us. He was still humming.

'That's some big omelette!' I said, when I saw it. It filled up the whole frying pan. 'How many eggs did you use?'

'About a dozen,' my father said.

'Mom only cooks one at a time,' I told him.

'When you taste this you'll know why I used them all up.'

'You mean it's that good?' I asked.

'Go on,' my father said as he served me. 'Taste it.'

I took a bite. It was awful! The worst thing I ever ate in my life. But my father was standing there grinning at me. I didn't want to hurt his feelings.

'Well?' he said.

'It's nice,' I told him, swallowing a chunk whole. I washed it down with a glass of milk.

'You see . . . your mother ought to experiment more. Then you'd learn to eat a lot of different things.'

'I don't think Mom ever made me a mushroom omelette,' I said.

My father put some on Fudge's plate. Then he served himself. Fudge shoved a lot into his mouth at once. I waited, figuring he'd choke on it. Instead he said, 'Oh . . . good!'

My father beamed. Fudge wasn't smart enough to fool my father. So he must have really liked it. But a kid that can eat flowers and swallow teeth wouldn't know much about omelettes anyway.

Then my father sat down and tasted his super-duper concoction. *He* not only choked on it. *He* spat it out! 'Oh no,' he said. 'This is awful. Something went wrong. Maybe the eggs are rotten.'

'Mom just bought them on Thursday,' I said.

'Maybe it's the mushrooms, then,' my father said.

'Maybe it's how you cooked it,' I suggested.

My father jumped up from the table and threw the mushroom omelette into the garbage. Fudge started to cry. 'Want more . . . MORE!'

'No,' my father told him. 'It wasn't any good.'

Fudge screamed, 'EAT IT OR WEAR IT . . . EAT IT OR WEAR IT!' He flung his spoon across the room. It hit my mother's favourite plant. The soil spilled all over the kitchen floor.

'Now you stop that!' my father yelled at Fudge. 'I'm going to make us nice peanut butter sandwiches. Then *you're* going to have a bath! Your mommy's coming home tomorrow and we're going to show her how well Daddy managed all by himself! Peter . . . where does your mother hide the peanut butter?'

After supper my father bathed Fudge. The only thing he decided not to do were the dishes. He stacked them in the sink and left them for my mother.

On Sunday afternoon we drove out to the airport to meet my mother's plane. On the way there my father said wouldn't it be fun if we kept all the things we did over the weekend a secret – just between the three of us – kind of a man's secret. I agreed not to say a word. And my mother was so glad to see us that she didn't even mention the dirty dishes in the sink.

Six weeks later we were watching TV one night when the new Toddle-Bike commercial came on.

'That's me,' Fudge said.

My mother looked up from the book she was reading. 'He does look like you, Fudge, but that's not really you.'

'Oh yes,' Fudge said. 'That's me . . . see . . .'

My mother squinted and looked harder. 'You know, Warren,' she told my father, 'he really does look like Fudge.' Then she laughed. 'Imagine another little boy like Fudgie!'

'It's Fudge all right!' I said.

'It's Fudge all right!' my brother repeated.

'We didn't tell you, dear,' my father said. 'We thought you'd like to be surprised. But that is Fudge.'

'WHAT?' my mother said, like she couldn't believe it.

'You see, Mom,' I began. 'Remember that weekend you went to visit Aunt Linda?' Then I stopped and thought about all the things my mother didn't know –

Like the puddles Fudge splashed in.
And the paper towels up his pants.
And how he wanted to touch the bears.
And the mushroom omelette.
And Mr. Vincent and his big cigar.
And Janet and her goldfish crackers.

And I looked at my father and I started to laugh. So did he.

– 10 –
Dribble!

I will never forget Friday, May tenth. It's the most important day of my life. It didn't start out that way. It started out ordinary. I went to school. I ate my lunch. I had gym. And then I walked home from school with Jimmy Fargo. We planned to meet at our special rock in the park as soon as we changed our clothes.

In the elevator I told Henry I was glad summer was coming. Henry said he was too. When I got out at my floor I walked down the hall and opened the door to my apartment. I took off my jacket and hung it in the closet. I put my books on the hall table next to my mother's purse. I went straight to my room to change my clothes and check Dribble.

The first thing I noticed was my chain latch. It was unhooked. My bedroom door was open. And there was a chair smack in the middle of my doorway. I nearly tumbled over it. I ran to my dresser to check Dribble. He wasn't there! His bowl with the rocks and water was there – but Dribble was gone.

I got really scared. I thought, *Maybe he died while I was at school and I didn't know about it.* So I rushed into the kitchen and hollered, 'Mom . . . where's Dribble?' My mother was baking something. My brother sat on the kitchen floor, banging pots and pans together. 'Be quiet!' I yelled at Fudge. 'I can't hear anything with all that noise.'

'What did you say, Peter?' my mother asked me.

'I said I can't find Dribble. Where is he?'

'You mean he's not in his bowl?' my mother asked.

I shook my head.

'Oh dear!' my mother said. 'I hope he's not crawling around somewhere. You know I don't like the way he smells. I'm going to have a look in the bedrooms. You check in here, Peter.'

My mother hurried off. I looked at my brother. He was smiling. 'Fudge, do you know where Dribble is?' I asked calmly.

Fudge kept smiling.

'Did you take him? Did you, Fudge?' I asked not so calmly.

Fudge giggled and covered his mouth with his hands. I yelled. 'Where is he? What did you do with my turtle?'

No answer from Fudge. He banged his pots and pans together again. I yanked the pots out of his hand. I tried to speak softly. 'Now tell me where Dribble is. Just tell me where my turtle is. I won't be mad if you tell me. Come on, Fudge . . . please.'

Fudge looked up at me. 'In tummy,' he said.

'What do you mean, in tummy?' I asked, narrowing my eyes.

'Dribble in tummy!' he repeated.

'What tummy?' I shouted at my brother.

'This one,' Fudge said, rubbing his stomach. 'Dribble in this tummy! Right here!'

I decided to go along with his game. 'Okay. How did he get in there, Fudge?' I asked.

Fudge stood up. He jumped up and down and sang

out, 'I ATE HIM . . . ATE HIM . . . ATE HIM!' Then he ran out of the room.

My mother came back into the kitchen. 'Well, I just can't find him anywhere,' she said. 'I looked in all the dresser drawers and the bathroom cabinets and the shower and the bath and . . .'

'Mom,' I said, shaking my head. 'How could you?'

'How could I what, Peter?' Mom asked.

'How could you let him do it?'

'Let who do what, Peter?' Mom asked.

'LET FUDGE EAT DRIBBLE!' I screamed.

My mother started to mix whatever she was baking. 'Don't be silly, Peter,' she said. 'Dribble is a turtle.'

'HE ATE DRIBBLE!' I insisted.

'*Peter Warren Hatcher!* STOP SAYING THAT!' Mom hollered.

'Well, ask him. Go ahead and ask him,' I told her.

Fudge was standing in the kitchen doorway with a big grin on his face. My mother picked him up and patted his head. 'Fudgie,' she said to him, 'tell Mommy where brother's turtle is.'

'In tummy,' Fudge said.

'What tummy?' Mom asked.

'MINE!' Fudge laughed.

My mother put Fudge down on the kitchen counter where he couldn't get away from her. 'Oh, you're fooling Mommy . . . right?'

'No fool!' Fudge said.

My mother turned very pale. 'You really ate your brother's turtle?'

Big smile from Fudge.

'YOU MEAN THAT YOU PUT HIM IN YOUR

MOUTH AND CHEWED HIM UP . . . LIKE THIS?'
Mom made believe she was chewing.

'No,' Fudge said.

A smile of relief crossed my mother's face. 'Of course
you didn't. It's just a joke.' She put Fudge down on the
floor and gave me a *look*.

Fudge babbled. 'No chew. No chew. Gulp . . . gulp
. . . all gone turtle. Down Fudge's tummy.'

Me and my mother stared at Fudge.

'You didn't!' Mom said.

'Did so!' Fudge said.

'No!' Mom shouted.

'Yes!' Fudge shouted back.

'Yes?' Mom asked weakly, holding onto a chair with
both hands.

'Yes!' Fudge beamed.

My mother moaned and picked up my brother. 'Oh
no! My angel! My precious little baby! OH . . . NO . . .'

My mother didn't stop to think about my turtle. She
didn't even give Dribble a thought. She didn't even stop
to wonder how my turtle liked being swallowed by my
brother. She ran to the phone with Fudge tucked under
one arm. I followed. Mom dialled the operator and
cried, 'Oh help! This is an emergency. My baby ate a turtle . . . STOP THAT LAUGHING,' my mother told the
operator. 'Send an ambulance right away; 25 West 68th
Street.'

Mom hung up. She didn't look too well. Tears were
running down her face. She put Fudge down on the
floor. I couldn't understand why she was so upset. Fudge
seemed just fine.

'Help me, Peter,' Mom begged. 'Get me blankets.'

I ran into my brother's room. I grabbed two blankets from Fudge's bed. He was following me around with that silly grin on his face. I felt like giving him a pinch. How could he stand there looking so happy when he had my turtle inside him?

I delivered the blankets to my mother. She wrapped Fudge up in them and ran to the front door. I followed and grabbed her purse from the hall table. I figured she'd be glad I thought of that.

Out in the hall I pressed the elevator buzzer. We had to wait a few minutes. Mom paced up and down in front of the elevator. Fudge was cradled in her arms. He sucked his fingers and made that slurping noise I like. But all I could think of was Dribble.

Finally, the elevator got to our floor. There were three people in it besides Henry. 'This is an emergency,' Mom wailed. 'The ambulance is waiting downstairs. Please hurry!'

'Yes, Mrs. Hatcher. Of course,' Henry said. 'I'll run her down just as fast as I can. No other stops.'

Someone poked me in the back. I turned around. It was Mrs. Rudder. 'What's the matter?' she whispered.

'It's my brother,' I whispered back. 'He ate my turtle.'

Mrs. Rudder whispered *that* to the man next to her and *he* whispered it to the lady next to *him* who whispered it to Henry. I faced front and pretended I didn't hear anything.

My mother turned around with Fudge in her arms and said, 'That's not funny. Not funny at all!'

But Fudge said, 'Funny, funny, funny Fudgie!'

Everybody laughed. Everybody except my mother.

The elevator door opened. Two men, dressed in

white, were waiting with a stretcher. 'This the baby?' one of them asked.

'Yes. Yes, it is,' Mom sobbed.

'Don't worry, lady. We'll be at the hospital in no time.'

'Come, Peter,' my mother said, tugging at my sleeve. 'We're going to ride in the ambulance with Fudge.'

My mother and I climbed into the back of the blue ambulance. I was never in one before. It was neat. Fudge kneeled on a cot and peered out through the window. He waved at the crowd of people that had gathered on the sidewalk.

One of the attendants sat behind with us. The other one was driving. 'What seems to be the trouble, lady?' the attendant asked. 'This kid looks pretty healthy to me.'

'He swallowed a turtle,' my mother whispered.

'He did WHAT?' the attendant asked.

'Ate my turtle. That's what!' I told him.

My mother covered her face with her hanky and started to cry again.

'Hey, Joe!' the attendant called to the driver. 'Make it snappy . . . *this* one swallowed a turtle!'

'That's not funny!' Mom insisted. I didn't think so either, considering it was my turtle!

We arrived at the back door of the hospital. Fudge was whisked away by two nurses. My mother ran after him. 'You wait here, young man,' another nurse called to me, pointing to a bench.

I sat down on the hard, wooden bench. I didn't have anything to do. There weren't any books or magazines spread out, like when I go to Dr. Cone's office. So I

watched the clock and read all the signs on the walls. I
found out I was in the emergency section of the hospital.

After a while the nurse came back. She gave me some
paper and crayons. 'Here you are. Be a good boy and
draw some pictures. Your mother will be out soon.'

I wonder if she knew about Dribble and that's why
she was trying to be nice to me. I didn't feel like drawing
any pictures. I wondered what they were doing to Fudge
in there. Maybe he wasn't such a bad little guy after all.
I remembered that Jimmy Fargo's little cousin once
swallowed the most valuable rock from Jimmy's collec-
tion. And my mother told me that when I was a little kid
I swallowed a quarter. Still . . . a quarter's not like a
turtle!

I watched the clock on the wall for an hour and ten
minutes. Then a door opened and my mother stepped
out with Dr. Cone. I was surprised to see him. I didn't
know he worked in the hospital.

'Hello, Peter,' he said.

'Hello, Dr. Cone. Did you get my turtle?'

'Not yet, Peter,' he said. 'But I do have something to
show you. Here are some X-rays of your brother.'

I studied the X-rays as Dr. Cone pointed things out to
me.

'You see,' he said. 'There's your turtle . . . right there.'

I looked hard. 'Will Dribble be in there forever?' I
asked.

'No. Definitely not! We'll get him out. We gave Fudge
some medicine already. That should do the trick nicely.'

'What kind of medicine?' I asked. 'What trick?'

'Castor oil, Peter,' my mother said. 'Fudge took castor
oil. And milk of magnesia. And prune juice too. Lots of

that. All those things will help to get Dribble out of Fudge's tummy.'

'We just have to wait,' Dr. Cone said. 'Probably until tomorrow or the day after. Fudge will have to spend the night here. But I don't think he's going to be swallowing anything that he isn't supposed to be swallowing from now on.'

'How about Dribble?' I asked. 'Will Dribble be all right?' My mother and Dr. Cone looked at each other. I knew the answer before he shook his head and said, 'I think you may have to get a new turtle, Peter.'

'I don't want a new turtle!' I said. Tears came to my eyes. I was embarrassed and wiped them away with the back of my hand. Then my nose started to run and I had to sniffle. 'I want Dribble.' I said. 'That's the only turtle I want.'

My mother took me home in a taxi. She told me my father was on his way to the hospital to be with Fudge. When we got home she made me lamb chops for dinner, but I wasn't very hungry. My father came home late that night. I was still up. My father looked gloomy. He whispered to my mother, 'Not yet . . . nothing yet.'

The next day was Saturday. No school. I spent the whole day in the hospital waiting room. There were plenty of people around. And magazines and books too. It wasn't like the hard bench in the emergency hallway. It was more like a living room. I told everybody that my brother ate my turtle. They looked at me kind of funny. But nobody ever said they were sorry to hear about my turtle. Never once.

My mother joined me for supper in the hospital coffee

shop. I ordered a hamburger but I left most of it. Because right in the middle of supper my mother told me that if the medicine didn't work soon Fudge might have to have an operation to get Dribble out of him. My mother didn't eat anything.

That night my grandmother came to stay with me. My mother and father stayed at the hospital with Fudge. Things were pretty dreary at home. Every hour the phone rang. It was my mother calling from the hospital with a report.

'Not yet . . . I see,' Grandma repeated. 'Nothing happening yet.'

I was miserable. I was lonely. Grandma didn't notice. I even missed Fudge banging his pots and pans together. In the middle of the night the phone rang again. It woke me up and I crept out into the hallway to hear what was going on.

Grandma shouted, 'Whoopee! It's out! Good news at last.'

She hung up and turned to me. 'The medicine has finally worked, Peter. All that castor oil and milk of magnesia and prune juice finally worked. The turtle is out!'

'Alive or dead?' I asked.

'PETER WARREN HATCHER, WHAT A QUESTION!' Grandma shouted.

So my brother no longer had a turtle inside of him. And I no longer had a turtle! I didn't like Fudge as much as I thought I did before the phone rang.

The next morning Fudge came home from the hospital. My father carried him into the apartment. My mother's arms were loaded with presents. All for Fudge! My mother put the presents down and kissed him. She said, 'Fudgie can have anything he wants. Anything at all. Mommy's so happy her baby's all better!'

It was disgusting. Presents and kisses and attention for Fudge. I couldn't even look at him. He was having fun! He probably wasn't even sorry he ate my turtle.

That night my father came home with the biggest box of all. It wasn't wrapped up or anything but I knew it was another present. I turned away from my father.

'Peter,' he said. 'This box is a surprise for you!'

'Well, I don't want another turtle,' I said. 'Don't think you can make me feel better with another turtle . . . because you can't.'

'Who said anything about a turtle, son?' Dad asked. 'You see, Peter, your mother and I think you've been a good sport about the whole situation. After all, Dribble *was* your pet.'

I looked up. Could I be hearing right? Did they really remember about me and Dribble? I put my hand inside the box. I felt something warm and soft and furry. I knew it was a dog, but I pretended to be surprised when he jumped up on my lap and licked me.

Fudge cried. 'Ohhh . . . doggie! See . . . doggie!' He ran right over and grabbed my dog's tail.

'Fudge,' my father said, taking him away. 'This is your brother's dog. Maybe someday you'll have a dog of your own. But this one belongs to Peter. Do you understand?'

Fudge nodded. 'Pee-tah's dog.'

'That's right,' my father said. 'Peter's dog!' Then he turned to me. 'And just to be sure, son,' he said, 'we got a dog that's going to grow quite big. *Much* too big for your brother to swallow!'

We all laughed. My dog was neat.

I named him Turtle . . . . to remind me.